CAMP SYLVANIA

ALSO BY JULIE MURPHY

TEEN NOVELS

Side Effects May Vary
Ramona Blue
Dumplin'
Puddin'
Pumpkin
Faith: Taking Flight
Faith: Greater Heights

MIDDLE GRADE NOVELS

Dear Sweet Pea

CAMP SYLVANIA

JULIE MURPHY

BALZER + BRAY

An Imprint of HarperCollins*Publishers*

Balzer + Bray is an imprint of HarperCollins Publishers.

Camp Sylvania
Copyright © 2023 by Julie Murphy
Lettering © 2023 by Alix Northrup
Map © 2023 by Steph Waldo
Interior illustrations by Jenna Stempel-Lobell
All rights reserved. Printed in the United States of America.
No part of this book may be used or reproduced in any manner
whatsoever without written permission except in the case of brief
quotations embodied in critical articles and reviews.
For information address HarperCollins Children's Books,
a division of HarperCollins Publishers, 195 Broadway, New York, NY 10007.
www.harpercollinschildrens.com

Library of Congress Control Number: 2022947978
ISBN 978-0-06-311402-9

Typography by Jenna Stempel-Lobell
23 24 25 26 27 LBC 5 4 3 2 1
First Edition

For all the kids—and kids at heart—
with big bones and big dreams

Dear Grandma,
someone once said, "War is hell."
They've never been to fat camp.
—From the movie *Heavyweights*

THE LAST DAY OF FIFTH GRADE

CHAPTER ONE

Fifth grade is officially history.

I love the last day as much as the next kid, but this particular last day of school is even more special, because this is *it*. This is the summer that I've waited my whole life for. This is *the* summer.

My classmates rush past me as I linger by the door, waiting for Nora as she carefully double-checks her desk for any remaining pens or notebooks. My best friend is very serious about writing utensils and paper products. Her notes are so perfectly color coded that they make me wish I could force my brain to be as organized as hers.

Instead, I'm the kind of person who regularly loses new notebooks after only using up a few pages and somehow always manages to misplace every pencil I own. But maybe that's why Nora and I are the best kind of friends. As long as we stick together, I have someone to borrow a pen from . . . and she has someone to save her from her older brothers.

Nora checks her bag and then pats her pockets, just like my dad does when he's about to leave the house, before turning on her heel and marching toward me.

"Are you ready?" I ask as I push my glasses up my nose.

"Yup, I think that's everything," she says as we wave goodbye to Mr. Stickney as he kicks his feet up on his desk and tears open a bag of Twizzlers. He holds his energy drink up as if he's cheers-ing us—and his kid-free summer.

"No," I tell Nora. "I mean, are you ready for the best summer of our lives?"

The fourth grader in front of us opens his binder and throws every single sheet of paper in the air.

As the loose pages cascade all around us, Nora presses down on the top of her pen, clicking it shut, before tucking it away in the side pocket of her backpack. "I was born ready."

I loop my arm through hers and we take off in a run down the hallway, willfully breaking one of the strictest rules of Pierson Elementary: NO RUNNING. But not a single teacher calls after us to stop, which means it really is officially summer.

"Camp Rising Star, here we come!" I yell.

"Woo-hoo!" Nora howls as we walk right out the door.

After escaping the chaos of Pierson Elementary, Nora and I take the long way home, so we can make plans for our three weeks away at Camp Rising Star. Not only are we finally going to the camp of our dreams, but we're doing it together!

"We should pack our matching T-shirts," Nora says with certainty. "The ones with the blue stripes and the flamingos."

"Maybe I should ask my dad if he'll buy us walkie-talkies," I muse. "Just in case we don't get assigned to the same cabin."

She shakes her head. "Don't say that, Mags. The emails with bunk assignments go out tonight. For all we know, you could be jinxing us."

I shrug. "The decision is probably already made. Unless someone hacks the camp email address."

"Wait. We can do that?" Nora asks.

I snort at the thought. "I'm not even allowed to have a cell phone yet, so I'm going with a no on that one." If it were as easy as that, I would have found a way to bump our names up the Camp Rising Star wait list that we've been on for three years before finally getting accepted this year.

She shrugs. "Tightrope practice?"

"Heck yeah!"

Nora skips to the other side of the street, so that we each have our own sidewalk as we pretend to walk our own tightrope along the curb. She holds her sundress up so that it doesn't get in the way. Not only is Nora Anne Whaley my very best friend, she's also talented like *whoa* and so fashionable that even middle schoolers and sometimes high schoolers compliment her when we're at the mall or the movies. She somehow coordinates her outfits to the bands on her braces and has a different pair of tennis shoes for every day of the week—possibly even the month. She always wears her curly dark brown hair in a French braid or down with a statement headband.

"Do you really think we'll be able to do real circus tricks by the end of the summer?" Nora asks from the other side of Sweet Corn Lane.

"That's what the website says," I tell her. "I wonder if my mom will let me order a few leotards. I don't want to show up to jazz and tap in regular gym clothes. I want to look like a professional."

She nods as we both approach the end of the street. "Dress for success."

Sweet Corn Lane dead-ends into our street, Plum Tree Drive. I peer down my end of the block, where Mom's and Dad's cars are both parked. That's weird. Dad is a horror novelist and works from home, but Mom is usually stuck in traffic on her way home from the hospital until almost dinnertime.

"I'll call you after supper," Nora says as she turns down her side of the street.

"Okay. We need to start thinking about how we want to decorate our cabin," I call after her. "I want to make a statement . . . and not the one my actual room makes, which is: sometimes I go to bed in my school clothes so that I can sleep in a little bit and everything on my walls is hung up with tape because my mom won't let me put holes in the wall."

She rubs her hands together with excitement. "Oooooh!

The possibilities! Maybe I can bring my Blackpink posters. . . .
I still have my Playbills from *Hamilton* and *Mean Girls* that
we could hang up too. . . . Bye for now, Magpie!"

"Bye for now, NorBear!" I call back.

As I walk past the first three houses on my end of our
road, I cut across the street to my yard.

We moved here the summer after first grade from the
other side of town, so not only was I getting a new house but
also a new school and, if I was lucky, new friends.

I spotted Nora, a girl my age and size with light brown
skin, on moving day. She was outside with her older brothers, who were eleven and thirteen at the time and hated that
their mom always made them let Nora tag along. To be honest, I'm pretty sure Nora didn't like it either. She kept peeling
off from them while they played basketball in the cul-de-sac
and would ride her bike down to my end of the street.

I remember my stomach fluttering every time she would
ride past my house, make a loop, and then go back down
the street. Surely if we lived this close to each other, we'd
go to the same school, and if I could muster the courage to
talk to her, I might just start my first day with a friend right
off the bat.

Before Nora, I'd never really had a friend—or at least a
friend I could call my own. Every kid I hung out with before
her was because my parents knew their parents or because
the whole class was invited to a birthday party.

On moving day, Mom was directing the movers and telling

them what rooms to put what furniture in when I finally walked out into the middle of the road and announced, "Did you know that some circus performers ride a bike with only one wheel? It's called a unicycle." Probably not the smoothest first line, but it didn't matter because Nora and I turned out to be the exact same kind of nerds.

Her feet dropped to the ground as she steadied herself. "You've been to a circus before?"

"Not one with animals," I clarified. "Mom says they used to have animals, but that it was actually a pretty bad deal for them."

"Was it fun? I'm sort of scared of clowns," she admitted.

I nodded. "The clowns were a little creepy but mostly funny. Their costumes were actually kind of cool. Do you want to see my souvenirs?" I asked.

She called down to her brothers, who barely noticed that she was going inside with me, her new friend. And that was that. *Friends.* Eventually friends turned into best friends, and now we're inseparable, with big plans to become real, honest-to-God actresses. And it all starts this summer!

If I can just get over my stage fright.

Last year we played orphans in the Sunnyvale Community Theatre Day Camp's production of *Annie.* Nora was Annie—*the* Annie!—and I was her understudy, which honestly had me uneasy from the start.

Don't get me wrong. I love theater. I love watching people perform, and . . . I want to love performing. I dream about it at night, and even during the day! But the moment I'm onstage by myself, my brain goes completely blank, like I've not only forgotten who I'm playing but who I actually am.

I audition okay, and I rehearse even better, but when it comes to performing onstage by myself, I clam up faster than an armadillo on the highway. That's why I prefer to be a chorus member or sometimes even a stagehand. In fact, I like to think of myself as Nora's very own personal backup singer. And even big Broadway shows and Hollywood movies need chorus members and extras! Not everyone can be the star . . . and that's okay.

The moment I saw the *Annie* cast list and I saw that I was her understudy, panic washed over me. Nora swore to me she wouldn't ever need me to step in for her and that being her understudy just meant we had more time to hang out together.

Well, that was fine and dandy, except her promise was only half-true. We hung out together every waking hour, but neither of us could have predicted that she would get a nasty case of food poisoning after a shrimp cocktail gone wrong at her dad's birthday dinner the night before our second-to-last performance. As for how I did . . . I'll just say that the day camp director said he'd never seen such a "robotic interpretation" of Annie before. And I don't think he meant that as a compliment.

But all of that is behind us now, and Nora and I are going to meet our destiny at Camp Rising Star. With that many talented kids in one place, there's no way I'll get cast as a lead or even nab a speaking role. I'll get to do the thing I dream of without the weight of the show resting on my shoulders!

The thought alone sets off fireworks of excitement inside me. There's a skip in my step as I open the front door.

Our tan-and-white corgi, Pickle, is waiting for me. He seems to look past me, like he's wondering where Nora, his second favorite person in the world, is. "She had to go home, buddy," I tell him.

"Mom?" I call, noticing her purse hanging on the banister. "Is everything okay?"

"In here, hon!" Dad says from his office upstairs.

I race up the steps with Pickle on my heels and drop my bag on the landing. "Coming!"

Dad is sitting behind his desk with stacks of old and new manuscripts all around him like little anthills. He says the chaos of his desk makes sense to him, but I find that hard to believe, considering most of the pages are covered in coffee mug stains and some are even from books he published years ago. The disorganized shelves behind him are practically toppling with books and collectible figurines from all kinds of things, like old swamp-creature movies and *Star Wars*.

Mom sits in his armchair still in her scrubs from work. The small tattoo, a paper airplane she and Dad both got on their wedding night, peeks out from the hem of her shirt-sleeve. She looks tired, like it's been a long day of running up and down the halls of the hospital, but she's definitely vibrating with energy like she is on Christmas morning when she's waiting for me and Dad (the family sleepyheads) to make our way downstairs for presents.

"Did you get the email?" I ask them both. "From Camp Rising Star? About bunk assignments?"

"Well, good afternoon to you too," Mom says with a grin.

I roll my eyes and run over to give her a quick hug before perching on the arm of the chair. "What are you doing home?" I ask. "Slow day in the heart business?"

"What are you?" she asks. "My boss?" Mom is a cardiological nurse, which means she helps people with heart health. She's always talking about step counts and heart-healthy diets, but she likes cuddling up on the couch and eating half a key lime pie by herself every once in a while too.

"Sweetie," Dad says, "we actually wanted to talk to you about your plans for the summer." He's in total deadline mode right now, so if we're having a family meeting in the middle of his workday, things must be serious.

"What's there to talk about?" I ask. "We've already sent in my tuition and forms for Camp Rising Star."

Mom places a hand on my knee. "Actually . . . we haven't."

I shake my head. "But—but I've been on the wait list there for two summers! What if I lose my place?" I point to Dad's phone on his desk. "Well, we have to call them right now. We have to call them and explain the whole mix-up. Is it the money? Did something happen with Dad's new book?"

Dad looks to Mom, like he's about to give in and spill

the beans. It reminds me of the time he almost ruined my big birthday present last year. (An electric scooter that I was obsessed with after seeing one just like it at Valerie Wilkin's slumber party. In fact, my dad is so bad at keeping secrets that he almost spoiled the ending for the third book in his Vampire Underground series during a podcast interview. Now his publisher has to approve every interview he does before it goes live.)

"The directors at Camp Rising Star were actually willing to hold your place until next summer," Mom says brightly.

I stand up, but then I feel immediately dizzy. My whole life has been building to this summer when Nora and I would finally live and breathe theater *and* with other kids who care just as much about the same things we do and aren't even embarrassed about it.

This is a bad dream. It has to be. What is she talking about? Next summer? What am I going to do? Sit at home alone for three weeks while Nora is off living our dream? I don't feel well. I think I'm going to be sick.

"Show her," Mom tells Dad as she turns to me. "Go look at your dad's computer. I think you'll be pleasantly surprised."

As Dad opens his laptop, I go to stand beside him, but my body feels like it's moving in slow motion through mud.

At the top of the web page in bold red letters, it reads, **CAMP SYLVANIA: A place for big dreams, big fun, and big weight loss.**

My heart sinks. Weight loss. Weight loss?

Of course.

For as long as I can remember, Mom has found ways to bring up my weight. Mostly it's small things like "oh that shirt is slimming" or whispering to me at a pizza party that two slices are enough. But sometimes it's bigger than that. Sometimes it's sit-down conversations about her wanting the best for me or being concerned for my health and happiness, or even worse, it's hushed conversations with Dad in the other room when they think I can't hear.

"It's baby fat," he said.

"It's not. You wouldn't know," she told him. "You were never big like I was."

Even when she doesn't bring it up, it's there in the way she watches me when I eat or how she makes me save old clothes that don't fit, because *you never know.*

And when it's not about me, it's about her. She thinks she's fat or her clothes don't fit right or her arms are too flabby. But the thing is—Mom is tall and skinny. If she thinks that about herself, what does she think about me?

On Dad's screen, below the **CAMP SYLVANIA** header is a slideshow of kids doing things that, I'll admit, actually look pretty fun. Bouncing off the inflatable blob in the lake, playing Marco Polo in the pool, racing go-karts, riding Jet Skis, and even performing in a play. Every last kid, though, is big. Not just big.

FAT.

RESULTS GUARANTEED it says in red flashing letters

that remind me of the commercial for a local car dealership that plays every night after the news.

SHED THE SHAME AND THE POUNDS! Sylvia Sylvania, the mind behind *Those Pants Make You Look Fat* and *Mind Over Body: Thinking Skinny*, is proud to bring you a new innovative fitness experience designed for the next generation. This summer it's time for your kids to unplug from their screens and power up with Sylvia.

"You . . ." I turn to them. "You're sending me to *fat* camp?" I should've known this was coming, but I'm still shocked. I didn't even know places like this still existed!

"Where does it say fat camp?" Mom asks. "It doesn't say *fat*. Don't use that word to talk about yourself, sweetie."

"But that's what I am, right? Fat?" I ask, my stomach involuntarily turning a little as the word comes out of my mouth.

"Honey," Dad says, reaching for my hand.

"I can't believe you made this decision without me," I say, my voice beginning to rise. "All I've ever wanted was to go to Camp Rising Star with Nora and you're stealing it away! Just because you're embarrassed of me."

Mom's jaw drops. "We have never in our lives been embarrassed by you, Magpie. We just want what's best for you, baby. You know I was a big kid too. It's not easy. Go to Camp Sylvania this summer, have an awesome time, and Camp Rising Star will be there for you next year."

My big dream of the perfect summer is slipping through my fingers like a melting ice cream cone on a hot day. "But . . . But what about Nora?" I ask. "We were supposed to go together. How am I gonna go the whole summer without my best friend?"

"Well," Mom says. "It turns out that Camp Sylvania is just down the lake from Camp Rising Star. You'll practically be able to yell to each other from the other side of the lake. And it's only three weeks!"

My chin begins to tremble. That's how I know I'm about to cry. And when I start, I won't be able to stop. "That doesn't make me feel better," I yell as I storm off down the hallway and slam my bedroom door shut.

Pickle chuffs, leaving his trusty spot under Dad's desk, before settling just outside my door as he guards me from my absolutely monstrous parents.

CHAPTER TWO

Any time I leave a room in a huff, my mom always lets me simmer instead of coming after me and demanding we talk, which is why I've been sitting here in my room for almost an hour and a half by myself.

Even Pickle gave up his post when he heard Dad opening his bag of dry food downstairs.

So many thoughts roll through my head. I can't go. I can't *not* go. Maybe there's still time. Maybe I can get my spot at Camp Rising Star back? And hardest of all, how do I tell Nora?

A folded pamphlet slides under my door, grazing my fingertips, as someone's weight settles against the other side.

I open the pamphlet to find vivid, colorful pictures of Camp Sylvania. The cabins are all painted bright pastel colors, and there's a huge barn with every kind of craft supply you can imagine. There's even a picture of some kids on a stage with costume pieces like hats and feather boas on over their everyday clothes.

"In case you want to read more about it," Mom says from the hallway.

"Or we could just rewind the last few hours and pretend it never happened and that my summer plans haven't changed," I call back to her.

"Maggie," Mom says softly. "You're not giving the idea of Camp Sylvania a chance."

"Why should I?"

She's quiet for a minute. "Hon, can I come in?"

I let out a loud groan and stand up to go sit on my bed. "Fine."

She opens the door, wearing her sparkly red glasses, my favorite pair of hers, and carrying a shoebox. After sitting, she sets the box down between us.

"What's that?" I ask with begrudging curiosity.

She opens the box, which is full of pictures from when she was younger. Maybe a little older than me, but before she met Dad the summer after high school.

I thumb through the photos and stumble upon a photo of Mom and two other white girls standing arm in arm underneath a huge arched sign that reads CAMP NEW BEGINNINGS. In the photo, Mom is still in what she calls her "chubby phase." The girl to her right is curvaceous with long blond hair, and the even larger, taller girl to her left has big brown curls that seem to have their own gravitational pull.

Mom and I look so much alike, especially when she was bigger. We both have the same unruly light brown hair. White skin with a pinky undertone that flares into red without much warning. But seeing this photo makes me feel like I'm only the before version of the person she hopes I'll become.

"Who are these people?" I ask.

"That's Birdie," Mom says, pointing to the woman with the brown hair. "And that's Sylvia. Sylvia Sylvania to be exact. They were my camp besties."

"You went to camp?" I ask. "And with the lady who *owns* Camp Sylvania?"

She nods. "Not just any camp. Weight-loss camp. Well, I guess they call it wellness camp now. But it's how I made it past my chubby phase. *Baby fat* is what your grandmother used to say."

I try not to roll my eyes. "Good for you, I guess? I just don't see why I can't go and be active at Camp Rising Star. They have all kinds of stuff. Dance class, swimming, and even yoga."

"Well, these are very special circumstances, Maggie. Me, Sylvia, and Birdie—the three of us loved Camp New Beginnings. We would email and text each other all year, just waiting to go back. But as we got older . . . and some of us lost weight, we stopped going and the camp . . . well, it got pretty run-down. In fact, it was nearly on the verge of closing."

"Really?" I ask.

"Until Sylvia and her company stepped in and bought the place just a few months ago. So, this is a really exciting chance for you to go to the same camp I did . . . sort of."

I squint down at the picture of them, focusing in on Sylvia, who, even through this photo, has serious popular girl energy. "Mom, is she—is that the woman you watch on YouTube? Is she the one who sells the protein shakes? That stuff you buy that tastes more like chalk than chocolate?"

She squawks at that, but still smiles a little. "It has the essence of chocolate, okay? And yes, that's the one!"

"Oh my god, so she's like famous *and* rich? And she's your friend? Do you get free protein powder? 'Nothing tastes as good as skinny feels—until you've had a Slender Like Sylvia Shake!'" I say, quoting the slogan from the commercials.

Mom shakes her head, laughing to herself. "No freebies. And yes, she is rich and famous. We were friends when we were younger, but we didn't stay in touch. I've been very proud to see all of her success. I just . . . Becoming friends with Sylvia changed my life. She really helped me lose the weight. She never stopped encouraging me . . . and now that she's bought Camp New Beginnings, I feel like I owe it to you to experience her magic for yourself."

"Or you could just send me to Camp Rising Star, where I might learn *actual* magic . . . ," I mutter, thinking about the stage-tricks class I saw on the sample itinerary. "What about Birdie? What did she do?"

"You know, Birdie and I fell out of touch too. I do think she worked for a few years as a counselor at Camp New Beginnings . . . but this isn't about some walk down memory lane. I wanted you to see this so you could understand that when your grandmother sent me to Camp New Beginnings, I was terrified." She flips through the photos of her smiling and laughing and doing stuff like Wild Hair Day or wearing pajamas to a bonfire. "But I made so many memories along the way," she continues as she grins sheepishly "And I lost all that weight."

I look down at the plumper version of my mother staring back up at me as she stands in front of a cabin with a big number three painted on the door. She's beautiful and glowing and confident and looks like she's got a joke on the tip of her tongue. I think she looks fantastic. Like the kind of person I'd want to be friends with or even the kind of person I'd want to *be*.

"But Mom," I finally say. "I think you were perfect then."

She pats my shoulder. "That's sweet of you to say, dear."

I don't know how to put the right words together to make her understand that she can't do this to me. She can't rip my dream summer out from under me.

"Honey," she says. "I remember what it was like to be . . . bigger. The taunting and the insecurity. It's not right, but the world usually judges the cover before they even give the book a chance. And I never want you to miss out on an opportunity just because someone was quick to judge you."

"Sounds like their problem," I mutter again. "Not mine."

But the truth is: I think about that a lot. Especially when I'm up there onstage all by myself without a whole bunch of other people to hide behind.

"Darling, it's my job as your parent to prepare you for that big, wide world out there. When you're here at home with me and your dad, you get to live in a bubble, but out there . . ."

"I know, okay? I get it."

She closes the box and scoots closer to me to put an arm around my shoulder.

I want to recoil, but it feels too good to lean into her. "So I guess there's no going back on this."

She leans her cheek atop my head. "Camp is paid for. One hundred percent nonrefundable," she confirms.

I let out a weighty sigh. How am I supposed to tell Nora I'm ditching her for fat camp? What if she goes to Camp Rising Star and makes a new best friend and realizes she doesn't need me like I need her?

What if this summer changes everything?

THE NIGHT BEFORE CAMP

CHAPTER THREE

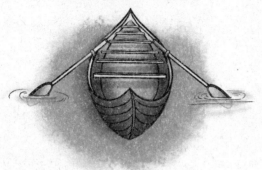

On the night before we both leave for our respective camps, Nora sleeps over. It was supposed to cheer me up, but I'm pretty sure it's having the opposite effect.

We lie on my bed with our heads tilted back, so that we can look out at the sky from the window.

"At least our camps are sort of close together," she says. "Maybe we'll find a way to meet up. Or figure out a way to send notes back and forth. Oh! Maybe we can meet on the lake in canoes."

When I broke the news to Nora she cried. And that made me cry. But in a weird way, it was nice to know that she was as crushed as I was to not spend the next three weeks together.

"If we don't drown trying," I say morosely.

I'd tried my very best to look on the bright side like Mom told me to over and over again, but even after a week of letting the news sink in, I couldn't see how missing out on

Camp Rising Star with my best friend had any bright side at all.

"That's what life jackets are for, Maggie."

"Tell that to the skeletons at the bottom of the lake," I say to her.

"There are no skeletons at the bottom of Lake of the Ozarks," she says, like she's trying to ward off a bad dream.

I turn over on my side, facing her. "That's not what my dad says. He says there's all kinds of stuff at the bottom of lakes, but especially Lake of the Ozarks. It wasn't always a lake. It used to be a place where people lived, but they released a dam and now there are all kinds of things at the bottom. Houses, cars, even swing sets."

Nora shivers wildly. "That's pretty spooky actually. Maybe we don't want to meet in the middle of the lake. At least not at nighttime."

We're quiet for a moment, letting the thought of what might lie at the bottom of the lake sink in before I whisper, "Nora, what if I don't make any friends at Camp Sylvania?"

"You make friends everywhere you go," she says. "If anyone has to worry about making friends, it's me."

"I almost don't want you to make friends even though I know you will," I confess. "In fact, I'm already jealous of all the friends I know you'll make."

She chuckles. "Like you won't make friends too!"

"Nora?" I ask. "What if I go to this camp and when I come home I'm still . . . well, the same size I am now?"

"Then I guess your parents will have to ask for a refund," she says with a snort before turning toward me and adding, "It won't matter either way. You'll always be Maggie."

I sigh loudly. "There's no way I'm falling asleep. I'm too nervous."

"Would it make you feel better if I told you I only had room for three pairs of shoes in my suitcase?"

"Now, that is actually tragic," I tell her.

"Let's play Would You Rather?" Nora offers through a yawn.

Nora knows Would You Rather? is my favorite and it always helps me forget about whatever is troubling me. "I'll go first," I say. "Would you rather only be able to drink like an elephant or have chicken tenders for fingers?"

"What if I ate my fingers?" she asks. "Would they grow back?"

"I mean, that would be cool, but you couldn't grow your real fingers back if you ate them, so no."

She yawns again. "I guess I'd drink like an elephant. I love chicken tenders too much and would probably eat my fingers before I even realized what I was doing."

"Fair point," I agree.

"Okay, I've got a good one," she tells me. "Would you rather live forever but never be able to go out in the sun like a vampire or sleep with your eyes open?"

"Ugh! Both of those freak me out big-time," I say, a chill running down my spine. "Well, living forever sounds fun, but what happens when all the people you love are gone? And I can't imagine never seeing the sun again. That sounds awful. But what about sleeping with my eyes open? Can I actually see what's going on around me? Or is it like only the people who see me sleeping know my eyes are open?"

Beside me, Nora is completely silent.

"Nora?" I ask. "Nora?"

I lean over so I can get a little closer to her, and it only takes a second to notice the way she's breathing in and out and her head has drooped to the side. She's out.

I flop back against my pillow and try closing my eyes, but my nerves are jumbled and I can't get my brain to quiet down.

Of course, I want to go to Camp Rising Star with Nora, but a very quiet voice inside of me wonders *what if?* What if I go to Camp Sylvania and I turn into a skinny mini and suddenly everything is easier? People are nicer. Teachers are sweeter. My jokes get funnier. I suddenly have the confidence to step into the spotlight all by myself. What if all along I was always meant to be skinny and this is the summer it happens? What if I'm not the fat girl? What if I'm just . . . a girl?

WEEK ONE OF CAMP

The freshly painted red letters on the side of the Camp Sylvania bus are bright and crisp except for where the *Y* drips down like it's bleeding.

"Hello, campers!" croons my camp counselor in the very tiny parking lot of the even tinier airport. When I imagined who might be waiting to pick us up at baggage claim, this woman definitely was not it. Her hair is damp like she just walked right out of the lake and onto the bus, but despite that, her big, bouncy curls look like they might just pop right out of her Chicago Cubs baseball hat. She's white with ivory tan lines where her socks slip down and she's cut out the collar and the sleeves of her Camp Sylvania T-shirt.

The counselor knocks a fist along the side of the bus, an old, rusty, but sturdy-looking thing. "Just rescued this beauty from the junkyard and gave her a fresh paint job. The camp doubled in size this year! I guess that's the Sylvia effect for ya."

Ugh, Sylvia. I'm not looking forward to many things about camp, but one thing I am completely dreading is whatever food Sylvia is going to attempt to feed us. If it's anything like her protein shakes Mom makes us drink for breakfast, I'm doomed. Moss-colored with a sludge-like consistency and it tastes just about as good as it looks, which is to say not at all.

The counselor, who is much stockier and broader than I expected anyone who works at a fat camp to be, stands on the first step of the bus and cups her hands around her mouth. "I am your recreational advisor at Camp Sylvania. You can call me Captain B. Today I am also your chauffeur. You will not criticize my driving unless you'd prefer to walk," she says with a chuckle. "Now, all aboard! Next stop: Camp Sylvania!"

The last time I was in a crowd of so many kids I didn't know was the first day of first grade, and even then, I knew Nora. A pit of loneliness settles into my stomach as I take the first step onto the bus. I wonder what Nora is doing at this exact moment. Probably meeting her bunkmates or going to orientation where you find out what show the camp is putting on.

I sigh inwardly. Fat camp, here I come.

As we packed my bag for three weeks away, Mom corrected me over and over again. "Maggie, it's not fat camp. It's a health and wellness camp." And I'd roll my eyes. Changing a thing's name doesn't change the thing.

On the flight here, I obsessed over the brochure my

parents gave me and I started to wonder if maybe this wouldn't be so bad. Maybe it would feel like all the fun days of PE combined. Like when you get to play with the rainbow parachute or have crab crawl races. But looking around at all the other kids—some of them bigger than me and some a little smaller—it's plain to see. We're the fat kids. And at some point, each of our parents decided that the extra fluff we are carrying is no longer cute. It's concerning.

One of the only remaining seats is up at the front next to a girl with deep brown skin, a peachy birthmark behind her ear, and her hair in a perfectly styled bun. Her pearlescent lip gloss glitters in the sun and her clothing is so proper, it might just very well be a school uniform.

"Come on and squeeze in with me," she says in an accent that I swear could belong to the Queen of England.

I can't stop my jaw from dropping. "You're English!"

She nods slowly. "You're American. And we're both fat . . . or plump if you prefer."

I slide my backpack under the seat and sit down next to her. "I . . . I've just never met an English person and I definitely didn't expect to find one here in the middle of Missouri at summer camp."

She shrugs. "Divorced parents. Summers with Dad in Kansas City means getting shipped off to fat camp for half my summer trip to the States."

"The website calls it a wellness camp," an Asian girl

28

behind us with jet-black hair and freckles splattered across the bridge of her nose says.

"Would it be weird if I asked Sylvia for her autograph?" the blond girl across from her asks.

My seatmate glances back at the first girl before turning back to me. "I prefer to call things precisely what they are."

"I guess not everyone is bummed to be here," I tell her. "And Sylvia has some fangirls."

"If I have to bunk with either of them, I might just bunk outside."

Up front, Captain B pulls the door shut. "Buckle up, kids!"

I begin to pat around my seat in search of a—

"Just kidding!" Captain B squawks out a laugh. "There are no seat belts."

"There never are on these American buses!" the girl next to me says.

"Righti-o you are!" Captain B sits behind the wheel and zooms out of the airport parking lot faster than any bus ever should. "Hold on to your butts, people!"

I grip the seat back in front of me with one hand and my seat with the other.

"I'm Evelyn, by the way," my seatmate says.

"Maggie," I shriek as we whip around a turn and down a narrow, tree-covered road. "I'm Maggie!"

"I'm Hudson!" the boy sitting in front of us shouts over the road noise. "Since you two are doing the introductions or whatever and apparently I'll have to talk to people in real life for the next three weeks since this place probably doesn't even have Wi-Fi . . . And this is my brother, Logan!"

I peer over the seat to see a barrel-chested, goth-looking white boy in black from head to toe with swoopy brown hair and his wrists stacked with black rubber bracelets. I immediately feel 20% less cool than him as he sits there with his nose in a graphic novel that has zombies splattered across the front. It's one I think I recognize from Dad's shelves.

Logan looks back and briefly smiles.

On our drive, Captain B teaches us a few camp songs, and every time the lyrics say Camp New Beginnings, she clumsily plugs in Camp Sylvania. "Camp New Be—Sylvania!" she sings. "You live in our hearts year-round and when we are afar, the memory of our bonfires warm us no matter where we are! Oh, Camp Syl-va-nia!"

I'm starting to think that maybe Captain B came with the camp when Sylvia bought it. Like a package deal.

Through the trees, I catch glimpses of the lake. We zoom past towering pine trees and smatterings of cabins as the water shimmers under the late-afternoon sun. The view is like a flipbook, the same scenery on a loop as we follow the winding road. When I looked up Lake of the Ozarks online with Dad, it looked less like a lake and more like a slithering river, but from here, it just looks massive.

Finally, we turn down a dirt road and under a sign for Camp New Beginnings, which has yet to be updated. Vines, leaves, and branches crawl up and around the weathered wood sign like it's being pulled back into the trees, and even though I know it's only my eyes playing tricks on me, it really does look like the branches are crawling over the letters. Below the sign is a bright and brand-new banner that reads WELCOME TO CAMP SYLVANIA.

Just as we pass under the sign, I notice a ghostly pale boy in neon-green swim trunks and tie-dyed tank top waving at us as he shakes his head, lips pressed into a thin, somber line.

I have to stop myself from shivering. "Do you see that?" I ask Evelyn.

But by the time she looks up, we've passed the boy . . . or maybe he's disappeared. "See what?" she asks.

I shake my head. "Nothing."

When the bus stops, I look out the window to see the camp staff lined up in all-white uniforms. White shorts, white polos with the letters CS embroidered on the chest, and a red belt. They're all equally slender and muscled, and none of them look anything like Captain B. They look like they're about to either perform surgery on us or star in a detergent commercial.

At the very end of the line is a thin, milky-pale woman with long blond hair, a flowy white dress, and a floppy red sun hat. Beside her, a man with perfectly styled dirty-blond hair holds a red umbrella over her head. In his other hand he holds a metal water bottle with a red straw for the woman in the dress to sip out of.

"Is that Sylvia?" I whisper, even though I know exactly who she is. If I didn't recognize her from all her photos and videos, I'd know her from the photo Mom showed me. She might be thinner and more polished, but something about her is still recognizable.

Evelyn squints. "She looks like she's allergic to the sun."

I shrug. "My mom's really into high SPF, so maybe it's like that."

As we unload, we're herded into a tight circle.

A counselor runs out in front of Sylvia and quickly opens a collapsible step stool for her to use. The same counselor also carefully replaces her sun hat with a headset microphone.

"Good afternoon, campers," she says in the same smooth and calming voice I recognize from her videos. "And welcome to the rest of your life. I think I can speak for my entire slim-and-trim team when I tell you that we are all thrilled to see what this summer holds, but first—let's get you settled into your new home. It's time to get acquainted with your bunkmates or as I refer to them: accountabili-buddies."

A rumble of excitement rolls through the crowd. Fat camp or not, roommates are the kind of thing that will make or break the next few weeks. I whisper a prayer to the universe in the hopes that my bunk luck is better than my summer camp luck.

CHAPTER FIVE

One of the counselors hands out maps to each of us with the camp rules on the back.

CAMP SYLVANIA RULES*

1. Curfew is nine o'clock. Sharp. Campers may not leave their cabins before sunrise.
2. NO contraband junk food.
3. NO swimming without a buddy and staff supervision.
4. NO cell phones, tablets, or laptops.
5. Counselors cannot enter camper cabins without being invited inside.

6. Obey Sylvia's Slenderizing System.

7. Or else.

* Rules are subject to change at Sylvia's discretion.

"Or else?" I ask under my breath.

Logan snorts without looking up from his book. "Or else she'll turn you into protein powder."

Hudson holds his head in his hands. "I can't believe how low-tech this place is. My DnD Discord is going to fall apart without me there to keep those peasants in line."

Logan leans over and whispers, "He didn't realize he'd be on a tech detox until our grandma took his phone, tablet, and laptop away just before we boarded the plane. He's still recovering and trying to figure out how to communicate to people without a screen to hide behind."

"I guess you're a fan of zombies?" I ask, motioning to his book.

"Any kind of horror, really," he says.

"My dad actually—"

"Attention, attention!" says a counselor in an all-white uniform who looks like a mini Sylvia, except she has dark brown hair and a slightly tan complexion. "My name is Sloane. And this is William." She points to the very tall and very unamused blond white guy next to her who had been holding Sylvia's umbrella and drink.

"Hi, Will!" Hudson calls, like a robot who was programmed to be human but isn't quite grasping human interaction.

"It's William," the man says in a serious voice. "Strictly William."

"William only answers to William," Sloane reiterates. "And don't forget it. We are your counselors and we'll be giving you a brief tour of the grounds and guiding you to your cabins. A little about me: I'm a micro-influencer originally from Mexico City. My inner child's name is Petunia. I've played a dead body on several television shows including *Grey's Anatomy*. I'm also a licensed hot-yoga instructor."

"I didn't realize they rated yoga instructors based on their hotness," an older white girl next to me with huge wavy hair says.

Evelyn holds her chin thoughtfully. "I'm pretty sure that's not what it means."

I smile at Evelyn like I even know what hot yoga is. "To be honest, I'm more concerned about the child living inside of her and how long it's been stuck there."

The other girl and Evelyn both snicker as we follow Sloane.

"A little about me," William calls from over his shoulder as he dramatically presses a hand to his chest. "I'm double-jointed. I've understudied in four Off-Broadway shows and performed on a cruise ship for three weeks before realizing I am tragically predisposed to seasickness."

"Did he say Broadway?" I whisper.

The girl with freckles sprinkled across her cheeks and her black hair pulled up into a tight ponytail leans over.

"Technically *Off* Broadway, but I guess that's still pretty impressive."

"Isn't every show that isn't on Broadway technically off Broadway?" I ask.

The girl nods thoughtfully. "You do have a point."

"I still can't believe they wouldn't helicopter you in and out every night for your shows on that cursed cruise ship," Sloane says under her breath.

William sighs. "I'm healing from a breakup this summer and am concentrating on stepping into my truest, most evolved self. Unfortunately, I'm also a certified lifeguard, but just because I can save your life doesn't mean I want to, so please be careful." He grimaces. "I'm really not looking forward to swimming in lake water."

They lead us all over the camp, which is built into a hillside full of pine trees and gravel paths. The cabins are much dingier than they were in the pamphlet, along with the other buildings, but I'll be the first to admit that the lake looks pretty epic. Just by the dock is a giant blob you can bounce off of. There are canoes and paddleboards along with the crown jewels—Jet Skis. Next to the cafeteria is a giant faded red barn.

"The craft barn," Sloane says, "also doubles as our theater where we'll have our summer musical on the last night of camp."

My heart stutters in my chest. A musical? Here?

"It's also where we'll have orientation tonight," she

continues. "You can drop off any mail outside the camp office right next to the cafeteria." She points to a faded lime-green shack with a screen door. "There is a total of twelve cabins and four sets of bathrooms and shower stalls."

"What's that for?" Logan asks, pointing to a fancy, sparkling white RV with a canvas circle-shaped tent just beside it.

"That is Sylvia HQ and it is one hundred percent off-limits," Sloane says in a very serious tone. "And the tent is for her daily sound baths."

"Is that like a bubble bath?" I mumble.

Evelyn shakes her head, because not even my brand-new super-fancy and cultured English friend knows what the heck a sound bath is.

Sloane leads us into the trees where tiny cabins dot the path. Each building has three beds and is lined with dark screen windows and canvas flaps that roll up or down. I'm dropped off at bunk three (Mom's same bunk!) with Evelyn (!!!) and the freckled girl who had been walking beside us.

"Hi!" the girl says as though we hadn't spoken just moments ago, and with enough nervous energy to soak up an entire room. "I'm Kit. Well, actually, back home I'm Katie, but I've been wanting to go by Kit for a while. I'm sort of nervous I might hate it. I thought camp would be a good time to test it out, ya know? Maybe I'm overthinking it. My dads say I'm a chronic overthinker."

I shrug. I'm pretty sure this girl's parents are right, but I'm not about to give her any more things to overthink. "Makes sense. Reinvention is very serious business. Just look at Taylor Swift. Anyway, good to meet you, Kit. I'm just Maggie."

"I'm allergic to mosquitoes," Kit adds.

"You do know that you're at a summer camp?" Evelyn asks. "This place is basically a spa day for mosquitoes."

Kit reaches into her backpack to reveal a plastic bag full of orange medicine bottles and aerosol cans. "That's why I'm fully stocked with prescription-strength bug spray and meds. Girl Scouts are always prepared. Especially ones with inconvenient allergies."

"You're a Girl Scout?" I ask. "Do you get employee discounts on those cookies?"

"I wish. One of my dads is my assistant troop leader and he's basically in charge of the cookies every year. No cookie goes unsold or discounted on Si-woo Choi's watch. My older sister was the troop's top seller before she quit to concentrate on violin."

"That's a bummer. About the discount," I say. "But cool that your dad is into Girl Scouts. Your sister too."

"My sister is basically perfect. She's skinny, smart, and plays the violin like an angel. She's no angel though; I know better. And Dad is an accountant who loves camping, so assistant troop leader is, like, his dream come true. My other dad—my white dad," she clarifies with a small laugh, "is super into pickleball, which I've tried multiple times and still don't get."

"Honestly, I'm not a big fan of any activity that requires score-keeping," I admit.

"Do you like musicals?" she asks. "Because you were talking about the whole Broadway thing. Sorry, it's just been a while since I've made friends with anyone and I feel like I want to know everything about you two. I mean, we are going to be living together for three whole weeks!"

"Musicals, plays, ballets . . . I love it all. Especially the costumes," I tell her. I like Kit. I like that she's nervous like me, but unlike me, she's not afraid to show it. "And I get it—who wants to live with strangers? It's honestly a relief that you two are normal—at least as far as I can tell."

Kit laughs. "You might be the first person to ever call me normal. What about you?" she asks Evelyn. "Do you have a thing or is being British pretty much your thing? Everyone I meet thinks being half-Korean is like my hobby or something."

Evelyn laughs. "This Black girl can relate. Like any good Brit, I like my tea, and I'm on the tennis team at school, but that's mostly because my mum signed me up. I don't get too much say in my free time, but that's what happens when both of your parents are barristers—or lawyers as you call them here. Sometimes I think every minute of my day is scheduled and negotiated. If it were up to me, I'd read all day. And write fanfiction all night!"

"Oh my gosh, you write fanfiction?" I ask. "My dad's a writer, but every time I sit down to write it feels so much like homework."

"Amen," Kit says.

"Your dad's a writer?" Evelyn asks. "Has he written anything I know? I mostly read mysteries . . . and my mother's romance novels when she's not looking."

I shrug. "He mostly writes horror novels, but his really popular series is called Vampire Underground."

"I saw those at the airport!" Kit says, obviously impressed.

"That is absolutely wicked. Is it weird to read his books?" Evelyn asks.

I shrink back a little with embarrassment. "Would I be the worst daughter ever if I admitted that I haven't read any of them yet?"

"That's fair," Evelyn tells me. "And don't tell your dad, but I think vampires are a bit of a bore."

"Your secret's safe with me," I tell her with a snort.

She breathes a sigh of relief. "Well, shall we settle in?"

Our tiny little cabin has three twin beds lined up in a row. I'm almost disappointed to not have bunk beds even though I secretly live in fear of falling off the top of one.

Kit claims the middle bed and Evelyn and I take a bed on either side of her. Evelyn hangs a British flag behind her bed, which she explains is called a Union Jack. Behind my bed I hang my collage of tickets and show Playbills from the touring Broadway shows that Mom and Dad take me to at the Bass Hall in downtown Fort Worth. And above Kit's bed is a star chart to help you identify the different stars and constellations in the night sky.

Looking out our screen window with a wistful sigh, I can almost make out the red-and-white big-top tent on the other side of the lake at Camp Rising Star.

"At least we're not at Opera Camp," Evelyn says as she places a framed photo of a hairless cat on the windowsill next to her bed. The charm on the cat's collar reads *George* in cursive.

I throw myself back on my bed. "There's a camp for kids who sing opera? There's a camp for *everything* and I'm stuck here! I was supposed to be at Camp Rising Star across the lake, but then my parents ruined that plan and sent me to fat camp."

"Me too," Kit confesses. "I'm supposed to be at Girl Scout astronomy camp, but I pulled out at the last minute because my grandma said she'd pay for me to go to Girl Scout camp and Space Camp next summer if I came here this year. She said it would help me lose my baby fat." She sighs. "I do get made fun of at school sometimes, though, so maybe if I just lose enough weight to where the bullies don't notice me, this summer will be worth it."

I know exactly what she means. Sometimes when I think about the future, I can only imagine a skinnier version of myself doing all the things I dream of. Starring in a show, traveling the world, saving the day, and maybe even falling in love one day. But then, I can feel myself getting riled up with every one of Kit's words. I don't want to spend my life hiding from bullies or suffering through a single summer at a place like this.

"What does *baby fat* even mean?" I finally ask. The phrase has always bothered me, to be honest. "And why are fat babies cute? At what age does it stop being cute?"

"And why do they call it *baby fat*?" asks Evelyn as she paces the room. "Because," she continues, "I'm pretty sure I've been on a diet since the day my mum and dad decided my fat was no longer baby fat. And—"

A loud chiming sound interrupts her. "Orientation begins in five minutes," an even voice says over the loudspeakers spread across the camp. "Please make your way to the craft barn."

My stomach growls. I hope they plan on feeding us soon.

CHAPTER SIX

The craft barn is nicer than any barn I've ever seen, but then again, the only barn I've ever seen in person was on my third-grade field trip to a donkey sanctuary and the whole place was a land mine of donkey poop. (I was pretty bummed to learn that the sanctuary was not actually a church for donkeys.)

Inside the barn, there are fairy lights strung from the rafters and giant spotlights strobe all over as we step inside. Lining the aisle leading to the stage are staff members, who are clapping in (and in some cases out of) tune with the music. I look all over for Captain B, but she's nowhere to be found.

There are rows of wooden benches, and at the end of the barn is a stage with heavy velvet curtains and a sign that says TODAY IS THE FIRST DAY OF THE REST OF YOUR LIFE.

"Uh, is that sign supposed to freak me out?" asks Evelyn.

Just as I'm about to answer her, the whole barn goes dark except for the strobing spotlights, which land on the velvet curtains as they're pulled open to reveal Sylvia floating down onto the stage with some seriously amazing harnesses we can't even see.

"Whoa," I whisper. This lady might be the reason my whole summer is ruined, but I can respect the theatrics.

The camp staff claps loudly for her and encourage all of us stunned, chubby campers to follow their lead.

Slowly I begin to clap as I peer back over my shoulder to catch Captain B lingering at the back before slipping out the door.

"Welcome, campers," Sylvia says into the same microphone headpiece she wore earlier today as the music fades. "I was able to greet some of you as you arrived today. How lucky—for me, but mostly for you. I see in you what I saw in myself at your age—a thirst! A hunger! A desire to unleash the thin person inside of you." Her voice reminds me of the preacher I see on TV sometimes who looks like he's about to tear right through the screen. Honestly, it's hard not to feel pulled in by Sylvia's every word. I think I get why she has so many loyal followers.

She sits down at the edge of the stage, and suddenly she doesn't seem like the wildly rich and famous person she's become. She just feels . . . normal. Like your really weird aunt or something, and I think I even recognize a little bit of the girl I saw in Mom's photos.

"Here's the deal," she says conspiratorially. "I know what it's like. And I'm sure you've all heard that from plenty of the adults in your lives. But I only say what I mean. So I really do know what it's like to wish you could fit in or fly under the radar. I know how it feels to think you shouldn't have to change to be seen for who you really are. But the truth is: the world doesn't change for *you*. You have to change for *it*, and what better time to make that change than right here and right now at Camp Sylvania!"

Something inside me lights up, like maybe she's . . . right. I look around and find I'm not the only one. Some are totally checked out, but a lot of us are hanging on her every word, hoping that maybe there's some truth to what she's saying.

"She wasn't even that fat," someone grumbles.

"What was that?" Sylvia snaps, standing up from the edge of the stage.

A girl in the front row with her hair pulled back into space buns puffs her chest out and repeats, "I said, you weren't even that fat. I've seen the pictures and—"

Sylvia lashes her arm out like an orchestra conductor ending a song. "We do *not* use that word at Camp Sylvania. The *F* word is explicitly off-limits."

The same girl throws her arms up with frustration. "If we can't say—"

Sylvia gives her the kind of glare that could drain the blood from your body.

I scoot back in my seat, gulping uncomfortably.

"—the *F* word," the girl finishes, "then what do we even call ourselves?"

Sylvia lists off a few options. "Rotund, plus size, husky . . . or my personal favorite: plump. You're smart kids. You'll think of something."

"Am I the only one who sort of likes the word *fat?*" Evelyn whispers.

"I never really thought much about it," I tell her.

Sylvia closes her eyes and breathes in deeply as she presses her palms together. She's silent just long enough for it to be awkward before finally opening her eyes again. "We have so many exciting things in store for you this summer. Tomorrow, we will begin our day by weighing and measuring every inch of you. We can't improve upon what we don't know."

On the other side of me, Kit shivers. "I hate when people weigh me."

And boy, do I understand. "At least we're all doing it together." Even though I can't decide if that makes it better or worse.

"Each afternoon, you'll be able to choose a recreational activity and tomorrow we even have auditions for the summer musical, which will be directed by Sloane and William with set design by B—Captain B. Participation in the musical hinges on your behavior and your willingness to participate in camp activities. You'll see the camp handbook being passed out along with some branded goodies sponsored by Sylvania Inc."

Bags are slowly passed through the audience. I peer inside mine to find my handbook, two red-and-white wristbands, and a matching headband that reads PROPERTY OF SYLVANIA INC.

Sylvia continues, "But most importantly, I believe in giving back, which is why each camper is asked to participate in the Camp Sylvania Blood Drive. You can donate up to one time a day. Bear in mind, this is also the only place on campus where you will be able to watch television and partake in contraband snacks, which are strictly for the sake of rebounding your blood sugar."

I choke back a gulp. "A blood drive? We're only kids. Can kids even give blood?"

Evelyn nods. "It's a bit odd, but blood transfusions *do* save lives."

"Very true," Kit agrees a little too loudly. "And they always give my dad a cookie and orange juice afterward."

Sylvia clears her throat as her gaze narrows on Kit, who shrinks down a little. "Some of you may have noticed that the camp rules included a warning that rules are subject to change at any moment. I'm new to life as a camp director, so any rule changes will be announced in the mornings or left outside your door."

She pauses for a moment as she waves forward a cameraman and a few other people. One of them carries a huge microphone. "Now, you might have noticed the camera crew following me around. This is Steve." She points to a tall balding white guy in a tan vest with tons of pockets. "This summer, they're filming a microdocumentary about me and my journey here, which will be used to promote my new book!"

Behind Sylvia, a spotlight finds a thick, glossy book displayed on a stand. As Sylvia reaches for the book, an image of the cover is projected behind her. The book is bright white with Sylvia in a vivid red, super-tight dress as she holds a raw bloody steak in one hand. The blood runs down her arm and onto the white glossy floor. It is both totally fierce and totally gross at the same time.

"The Scarlet Diet!" Sylvia beams. "A new, state-of-the-art diet—all inspired by the color red! The Scarlet Diet will be our guiding light this summer, and I'm so excited to share your meal plan with you starting tomorrow, which will also be served by our highly trained cafeteria workers." She motions to the side of the barn where the spotlight shines on three older women in once white but now red-stained cafeteria uniforms. One of them holds up a hand to block the light from her eyes while the other two squint.

"Those women look like they've been cleaning up a crime scene," I mumble.

Overhead, something rustles, and I can barely make out any shapes in the dark, but suddenly a small flock of birds swoops down and shoots straight out the barn doors.

"Were those bats?" Evelyn whispers.

"Barn bats are very common," Kit says with authority.

"The most wildlife I see at home is our neighborhood raccoon, Gigi," I tell them. "My dad leaves dog kibble out for her even though my mom says he shouldn't."

"Your neighborhood raccoon has a name?" Kit asks.

"My best friend, Nora, named her. We like to pretend she's a raccoon influencer who does, like, sponsored posts about the chicest trash in the neighborhood. We even went as influencer raccoons for Halloween one year." My cheeks warm with embarrassment at my total word vomit about the silly make-believe raccoon backstory I have with Nora. "No one else really got our joke."

Evelyn grins. "A trash panda who's also an influencer? That's quite funny."

Kit laughs. "That's pretty good."

I giggle at the memory of me and Nora in our furry costumes and gaudy jewelry. Something tells me she'd get along just fine with Evelyn and Kit.

Upbeat music begins to play and Cameraman Steve pans out to the audience as Sylvia says, "I hope you all get a good night's sleep. The real work begins tomorrow and there's no going back. Together, we're going to make the kind of lifestyle changes that will last for *eternity*!"

CHAPTER SEVEN

After orientation, my head is buzzing. Weigh-in, blood dona-tion, the weird no-*F*-word rule, and . . . a musical?

This is no Camp Rising Star, but there *is* going to be an end-of-camp musical. A musical!

Maybe . . . just maybe, I'll even audition.

The *Annie* understudy was a fluke if I'm being honest. Any other time I auditioned for anything back home, I was always cast as an extra. Well, except for the one time I was cast as George Washington's mother in a school play. I had one line. "George, please go pick some apples for apple pie." It wasn't what I would call inspired, but it also wasn't as tragic as *Annie*.

As the sun sets just outside, we're served brown bag meals in the barn since the cafeteria doesn't officially open until tomorrow. We're given sliced turnips, an apple, and roast beef and red cabbage sandwiches made with bread so crunchy and thin that it could be a cracker.

Back in our cabin, the three of us gather up our toiletries.

Mine are packed in a plastic baggie, Kit's are in an old pencil case, and Evelyn has a plush velour monogrammed pouch that unfolds so that it can be hung up on a hook.

"Whoa," says Kit as we walk out our door and to the restrooms up the hill, which we share with three other cabins. "Is that fancy bag just for your toothbrush?"

Evelyn shrugs. "And my skin care and hair care. Plus it matches my suitcase."

"My suitcase used to belong to my grandma," I say, referring to the old floral thing with broken wheels I had to drag through the airport. "But you're like some kind of world traveler, Evelyn. This is only the fourth time I've left Texas, and you're definitely the first British person I've ever met."

"Me too," Kit admits.

"The suitcase was my father's Christmas gift," Evelyn explains. "Well, really, it was probably my stepmother's idea."

"If your dad's going to make you go back and forth between London and Kansas City, the least he could do is a fancy suitcase," I say.

She nods. "Child-of-divorce perks."

A warm breeze rustles the trees overhead, and something flaps and hoots as it swoops so low above us that I almost duck.

"That must have been an owl," Kit says. "Though I'm not sure what kinds are native to this area."

"Um, I'm not really an outdoorsy person," I admit. "I mean, I like the outdoors, but I'm more of a sidewalk-in-the-park kind of girl than I am a woods-in-the-middle-of-the-night kind of girl." Earlier today, the restrooms felt like just a short walk. In fact, they're so close, I can see them from our screen window when the canvas flaps are rolled up. But in the darkness of night, this walk is a little farther than I'm comfortable with. In fact, I'm wondering if I should hold off on drinking anything after dinner just so I don't have to pee in the middle of the night.

"We're fine," Kit assures me. "It's not like we have to worry about coyotes or something. Black bears, sure. But we should be okay as long as we're not like hoarding any delicious, but totally against the rules, snacks."

I freeze. Was she snooping in my suitcase? "Um, I definitely did not sneak in some powdered donuts and gummy worms in the lining of my suitcase, but if someone did, should they be worried?"

Evelyn snorts out a laugh. "I'd be more worried about getting caught with contraband than I would be for a bear. But if I were really that worried . . . I might also be nervous if someone had snuck in some Jaffa Cakes and hid them in the secret compartment of their backpack."

Kit's gaze darts from me and then to Evelyn. "Are you two, like, talking in some kind of code or whatever?" When neither of us responds, she narrows her gaze on us before continuing to lead us up the hill. "Well, to whom it may concern, I would only worry about wildlife if the packages of said snacks are open."

Evelyn cackles.

"Ahhh," I say through a snicker. "Good to know. In a general sort of way, of course."

Kit whirls around on her heel, and for a moment I think she might just rat out me and Evelyn, but then finally she asks, "And what the heck are Jaffa Cakes?"

Evelyn groans. "Only the most delicious treat. Chocolate-covered biscuits with orange jam."

"I didn't even know biscuits could be dessert," I say, "but you had me at chocolate."

"Oh, there's a whole world of delicacies Americans aren't aware of!" Evelyn sorrowfully declares.

At the bathrooms, we find a line of girls wrapping around the small cement building with no ceiling, and my hands feel clammy already. I barely like peeing when other people are in the bathroom. Forget showering around other people. (It's honestly the thing that scares me most about middle school and high school.) With how airy these bathrooms are, I bet surrounding camps can hear you pee.

I wonder if Camp Rising Star has a better bathroom situation. All those years that I begged my parents to send me to camp, and I hadn't really considered that there might be some roughing it required. We might have cabins instead of tents, but bathrooms that require a flashlight to find might as well be in the wilderness if you ask me. I don't even have any siblings, so sharing two toilets and two showers with twelve other girls should be interesting.

As we join the tail end of the line, an older girl with wavy hair and light brown skin who I recognize from this afternoon is in front of us. She swats away a mosquito as she says, "I heard that if you sneak down to the docks at night, you can hear him crying."

"Hear *who* crying?" I ask, not even bothering to pretend I wasn't eavesdropping.

She turns back to us, her thick, bushy brows raised. "The camp ghost."

Beside me Kit gasps and I involuntarily shake my head. I like the idea of ghosts, like in movies or books, but the thought they might be real is the kind of thing that keeps me up at night. Especially when Pickle does things like bark at absolutely nothing in the middle of a room or at a dark staircase.

"The Weeping Boy," the girl says. "And if you get in the water at night, legend says you won't come out alive."

Tiny goose bumps run up my arms, and even though I'm not entirely sure, I boldly say, "It's not like ghosts are real."

"Maybe you should go down to the dock one night and prove it," she says in a voice that reminds me of Nora's taunting brothers.

"Charlotte! Stop trying to scare the babies," says a short, round white girl with boobs as big as my mom's. She wraps her wet hair in a towel as she turns the corner out of the bathroom.

"We're hardly babies," Evelyn says with authority.

"You're up," the other girl says to Charlotte before looking to me, Kit, and Evelyn. "I'm Tori and *babies* is, like, a term of endearment, I swear. That was Charlotte, by the way. She's just grumpy because of the takeover."

"The takeover?" I ask.

"This was supposed to be our last year at camp together," Tori says. "We've been coming here since we were in third grade."

"You've been coming here since the third grade?" Evelyn asks in shock.

"But you're still . . . big," Kit blurts.

Tori laughs so loud it scares even the crickets for a minute. "You didn't think people actually lost weight at fat camp, did you?"

"Sometimes they do!" Charlotte calls from the bathroom. "Remember Beckett from two summers ago?"

Tori nods. "Okay, sometimes. But until this summer, this place was super chill. There was hiking, water sports, crafts . . . it was a fat camp, sure—"

"Um, I don't think we're supposed to say that word anymore," Evelyn quietly inserts.

"Fat! Fat! Fat!" Charlotte shouts from inside the bathroom.

Kit and Evelyn both gulp in unison.

Tori rolls her eyes. "Don't want to get caught dropping the *F* bomb now, do we, Char?" She sighs. "Anyways, this Sylvia lady is going to ruin this place."

"At least Captain B is still here," Charlotte calls.

"Ladies!" yells an approaching counselor who I don't recognize but is in one of Sylvia's white uniforms. "No loitering after your showers. Straight to bed. Trust me. You don't want to be out here alone at night."

As the woman comes closer, I can see that her blond hair is slicked back into a severe bun and she is very petite, certainly shorter than some of the campers here. The name tag on her shirt reads *Helen*. Her skin is so pale it's nearly blue, the bags under her eyes are almost purple, and her cheeks are so sunken that her skin just looks like it's draped on her cheekbones. Basically, Helen looks like the kind of adult who thoroughly enjoys yelling at kids.

"Better get your fat butt to bed, Tori!" Charlotte yells as she turns off her shower.

Helen opens a small tablet she carries and begins to scroll. "Tori Gerber?"

Charlotte turns the corner, her wet hair dripping on the shoulders of her robe. "And Charlotte Buchanan," Helen adds.

"And you are?" Charlotte asks.

"I'm Helen. Your overnight counselor. You'll find me patrolling the grounds after dark, and if we happen to run into each other, it's safe to assume you're in trouble."

"You only work at night?" I ask.

Helen turns to me. "Is that a problem?"

I shake my head quickly. "No. No problem at all."

"Good." She spins on her heel and calls over shoulder, "Well, I suggest you all get ready for bed and back to your cabins before a problem presents itself."

When we get back to our cabin, Evelyn lets out a

bloodcurdling scream and so do I once I see the mouse sitting there on her bed.

"What's the commotion?" Kit asks, clamoring to see. "Oh, it's just a country mouse!"

The door slams shut behind us and we all jump—even Kit.

When I glance back, the mouse is gone. "I don't think I'm meant for camping. Even in cabins."

"Does there seem to be a problem?" a voice calls from outside.

We peer through the screen door to find Helen standing just outside the ring of light emanating from our cabin.

"Just a little old mouse," Kit tells her.

Helen steps into the light, shadows draping her cheekbones so that she looks sullen. "If you'd just invite me in, I'd be happy to exterminate that little pest for you."

Evelyn glances back over her shoulder to where the mouse was. "Uh, I think it actually ran outside, so we're fine."

"Yeah," I say. "Thanks for the offer."

"Very well," Helen says as she melts back into the darkness.

"That was creepy," Kit whispers. "Right?"

Evelyn and I both nod, and I try my best to ignore the anxious feeling bubbling in my tummy.

That first night as I'm falling asleep, I can hear Helen's footsteps crunching against the gravel paths as she walks up and down and up and down, and I swear I hear counting . . . or maybe that's just my brain tricking me into falling asleep. . . .

. . . nine . . . ten . . . eleven . . . twelve . . . thirteen . . .

CHAPTER EIGHT

Chirping birds are interrupted by the sound of a ringing gong.

"Good morning, campers," a smooth, lilting voice says into the loudspeaker that pipes into our room.

I pull my pillow out from under my head and pelt it at the speaker hanging above our door, but of course that does nothing and I'm just left pillow-less. A groan rumbles in my chest as I pull the yellow striped comforter I brought from home over my face.

"Is it really time to get up?" Kit asks.

"I've been awake for two hours already," Evelyn whines. "The jet lag is real."

"Please find activewear uniforms, amended camp rules, and today's schedule in a basket outside your door. Weigh-in begins at seven a.m. on the dot followed by breakfast, because who wants to get weighed on a full tummy?"

My stomach grumbles. "I wouldn't mind."

There is only one amendment to the rules so far and it's no surprise.

Amendment 1:

Usage of the **F** word is BANNED.

The big surprise however is the uniforms we're forced to wear. White bike shorts with matching tank tops that read FUTURE CAMP SYLVANIA SUCCESS STORY.

"My mother always says Americans have poor taste, and this uniform isn't helping anything," Evelyn says as she peers down at the red letters on her chest.

We sit on the ground under a huge canopy where counselors are lined up with very fancy scales, measuring tape, and some sort of awful device that's being used to pinch our soft stomachs. Off to the side, the camera crew races around, catching every angle.

Sylvia paces behind the scales, an assistant walking alongside her with a handheld electric fan.

"At least we have free time in the afternoon," Kit says. "Maybe we could go on a hike."

"I'm floating in that lake," I tell her. "No matter what."

"With the ghost?" she asks.

"I'll take my chances during the daytime."

I look up to find that there's only one more cabin before it's our turn. My stomach twists into knots. I hate getting weighed at the doctor's office. The nurses always frown as they write down the number and scribble some secret note about me. And even though we're all bigger kids, the thought of getting weighed in front of the whole camp has me breaking out into a nervous sweat. Sometimes when I use the bathtub in my parents' bathroom, I even put their scale under the sink so I don't have to look at it.

I don't know if I'm scared of what I weigh or what people will say about it. I've never looked at the number on the scale and felt angry or betrayed. But I have found myself, at the most unusual times, unable to think about anything else. I'll be lying in bed and those numbers will flash across my brain like a neon sign. Or sometimes I'm about to take a bite of my lunch, and those silly numbers are all I can see, and suddenly I don't feel like eating anymore.

"Cabin Three!" calls Captain B from her clipboard.

I take a deep breath and follow Kit and Evelyn.

Captain B steps in front of me. "Hey," she says with a warm smile. "Maggie, right?"

I nod.

"You okay, Maggie? You look like you might pass out. Do you need to sit down and maybe have a snack or something?"

"We can have snacks?" I ask.

Captain B's shoulders slump a little. "Well, Camp Sylvania sanctioned snacks."

"I'm okay," I tell her. "I just hate getting weighed."

She shrugs, like she knows just what I mean. "That's totally normal. Do you want me to see what we can do about getting you out of this?"

"I don't want to get in trouble," I say as a little sunbeam

of hope glows in my chest. Maybe if I just stick with Captain B and concentrate on the musical, this summer won't be so bad.

"You know what I do when I go to the doctor?" Captain B asks. "I get on the scale backward. The nurse writes down the number and I never have to see it, because I'll be honest: that number is no big whiff to me."

"Backward," I say. I can't believe I'd never thought of that before! "Yeah. Okay. I can try that."

When I go up front, I take Captain B's advice and step backward onto the scale.

Steve the cameraman notices what I'm doing and steps closer.

Sloane, who is tracking all my stats in her tablet, appears to be briefly confused before she says, "Have it your way. The number on the scale stays the same whether you see it or not."

"I know," I say firmly and with a smile on my face as the rest of the camp notices what I'm doing.

A few kids whisper back and forth and I wonder if maybe they're just as nervous as I am.

Sylvia saunters over to me, her lips outlined with a deep red lipstick.

My stomach flutters. For some reason I can't explain, I want her to like me. I open my mouth to ask her if she remembers Mom from their days at camp, but she speaks first.

"You can't fight what you can't see, my dear." She winks

at the camera and then she walks off to examine the next camper.

Maybe I don't want to fight against the number on the scale. But I bite back my words and am filled with relief when Captain B gives me two thumbs-up from the edge of the crowd.

I sit down again and as the rest of the campers are weighed, I notice that a few others take my lead and turn their backs to the scale.

"I wish I'd thought of that," Evelyn whispers.

After weighing in, we're sent over to the cafeteria. Last night, we were served boxed meals with salads and breadsticks that could hardly qualify as bread, but today is our first look at what kind of food we'll be eating for the next three weeks. Just like Sylvia promised, everything is red.

Apples, blood oranges, bacon, red smoothies, peppers, onions, cabbage, radishes, steaks . . . every red food you can think of. The only non-red offering is egg whites and thin, crunchy toast that looks rock solid enough to chip a tooth.

Just ahead of us in line, the blond Sylvia superfan from the bus yesterday turns to her bunkmates and says, "My mom says that Sylvia's new diet has basically broken science it's so good."

"I don't think I'm very hungry anymore," I say as a cafeteria worker with sunken eyes and nearly grayish skin slaps an omelet full of cabbage, onion, beets, and radishes on my plate.

"Does this even qualify as food?" Evelyn whispers.

"Maybe rabbit food," says Logan beside me.

And I swear the cafeteria worker hisses at him.

"I guess they're not a big fan of rabbits here," I say to him with a grin as we veer off the line.

Like the rest of us, Logan is in his all-white uniform, and it is so not his vibe that I almost want to apologize to him for having to wear it as he and Hudson follow the three of us to an open table.

Kit and Evelyn look to me with wide eyes and I know just what their expressions mean. A boy! Is talking! To one of us! Except I don't get all squirmy about boys. What's the big deal? They're just people and some of them smell like wet meat loaf or old tuna salad.

I mean, this boy doesn't. He smells like he uses body wash and the good kind that smells minty and fresh and . . . well, maybe he does smell nice. And he does seem a little bit mysterious.

"We met yesterday on the bus," Logan reminds Evelyn, and then to her and Kit, "I'm Logan and this is my younger brother, Hudson."

Kit and Evelyn giggle—for no reason!

I guess if I thought boys were cute, these two would qualify. They both have shiny brown hair and soft green eyes. Logan, though, has a touch of blond to his hair like it's barely been touched by the sun and his chest is broad and wide, like his whole personality lives there.

"Where's your book?" I ask.

Logan frowns. "I finished already and *someone* forgot to pack the rest of the series after I let them borrow it."

"Maybe the camp has a library," Kit offers, though she doesn't sound very hopeful.

"I said I was sorry," Hudson says with a groan. "I'm not the villain here, remember? If we were home spending the whole summer in the comfort of our air-conditioned basement or surfing down the street at the beach, it wouldn't matter that I left your comics under my bed. But our mom decided she just *had* to send us here after Aunt Nancy showed her the ad online. Now the only waves that lake is getting will be from the Jet Skis."

"Do you think we actually get to use those?" I ask.

Hudson shrugs. "It was on the website."

"Sounds like a death trap," Evelyn says.

I take a swig of my smoothie. "Mmmm!" At least something here tastes good. I hold the glass up. "What's in this thing?" I ask.

"It might be better if we don't ask," Logan says with a curled upper lip.

I can't help but laugh. At least it's better than the shakes Mom has us drinking at home.

"Who's your third bunkmate?" Evelyn asks them.

Hudson shrugs. "He disappeared."

"What?" I nearly choke on my food.

Logan rolls his eyes as he gently shoves Hudson. "He

didn't disappear. His name was Noah and he went home in the middle of the night. William said he was homesick."

"I feel that," I say with a sigh. "So you both really know how to surf?" I ask.

Logan nods. "I don't think you could technically call what Hudson does surfing, but yeah, I do."

Hudson flings a sliced radish at Logan's forehead, but he's unfazed.

"Where are y'all from?" I can't imagine living anywhere near the beach. Outside of Dallas–Fort Worth, there's nothing but flat fields until you hit the hill country or the desert or Galveston, I guess, which my dad says is a beach only in the technical sense.

"We're from Chula Vista, California," Hudson chimes in. "We have really good surfing."

"That's so cool."

"I could teach you," Hudson offers.

Logan gives his brother an impatient look. "Ignore him. He can barely stand on land. Forget a board. *I* can teach you. Maybe if they let us use the paddleboards here we could start with that."

"Cool." I can feel my cheeks warming, so I quickly look away and stare down at my plate for what feels like forever.

"Is anyone trying out for the musical?" Kit finally asks.

"Oh, not me," Evelyn says. "Maybe I'll see if I can help with props or something."

Kit chimes in, "I'm not much of a performer, but I would

help out backstage like Evelyn if I can."

"What about you two?" I ask Logan and Hudson.

"I've never been in a musical," Logan says.

"But Mom says he has the voice of an angel," Hudson blurts.

Logan's cheeks turn a deep shade of red. "Are you trying out, Maggie?"

I swallow back all my embarrassing stories and every feeling I have about being center stage and instead say, "Maybe for the chorus."

CHAPTER NINE

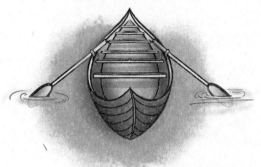

After the weigh-in and the weirdest breakfast I've ever had, we are led out to the edge of the lake where we are each assigned to Pilates machines that look like the kind of medieval torture devices I'd only read about when I did a presentation on the Tower of London.

As we're nearing the end of our workout with Sylvia in her all-white unitard, she tells us, "Now, stretch your body as long as you can. Think *lean* thoughts. Close your eyes and imagine the person you wish you saw in the mirror."

The only thoughts in my head are of air-conditioning and sleeping in so late that my first meal of the day is lunch.

The total silence is interrupted with a giant fart so deafening it practically causes a ripple across the lake. It's followed immediately by a smaller toot that causes us all to burst with gut-splitting laughter.

Sylvia clears her throat into her microphone headset. "Flatulence is simply negative energy vacating the body."

"That's the truest thing she's said yet," Charlotte says behind me.

I thought the Pilates torture machine under the beating sun was tough, but the thing that really kills us all is the uphill sprints William forces us to do while he stands under a shady tree and blows into his whistle over and over and over again.

After my fifth trip uphill, I plop down on the ground, feeling immediately dizzy.

"This. Stinks," I blurt between panted breaths.

Evelyn stands next to me, her chest heaving and a hand shielding her eyes. "Are those kids . . ."

I follow her gaze across and down the lake to where the lucky kids at Camp Rising Star are— "Having a water balloon fight," I finish for her as I wipe the dripping sweat from my forehead with the back of my forearm. The morning has sucked the life out of me and seeing the kids across the lake, including my best friend, having the time of their lives is enough to send me over the edge. "I gotta email my parents. I have to get out of here. I'd rather cut our lawn with scissors all summer than try to survive the next three weeks."

Evelyn lifts the front of her shirt to wipe the sweat from her forehead too before offering me a hand up. "Let's just survive until lunch and then we can hatch our escape plan."

"Okay," I say.

We take our time shuffling back downhill despite William's

persistent whistling, and two words get me through the rest of our sprints: ESCAPE. PLAN.

Forget the musical.

If I wanted some adult to just blow a whistle at my face for an hour, I could do that in PE every day at school. I gave it a fair shot like Mom asked, and now I'm getting out of this place.

But not before I ride those Jet Skis.

After lunch we are given precious, precious free time, and I'm a girl on a mission.

Back at our bunk, I change into my swimsuit, a pink bikini with bananas all over it. I begged and begged my mom for it when we saw it at Target last summer, but when it was time to wear it to the neighborhood pool with Nora and her brothers, I chickened out and swam with my T-shirt on over my beloved swimsuit.

When Nora and her brothers looked at me funny, I lied and said I burned too easily. Well, I guess it wasn't a total lie. Just a part lie. I do burn pretty easily, but that wasn't why I wore the T-shirt.

Before we leave for the lake, I reach into my suitcase for my trusty T-shirt, but when I look up Kit and Evelyn are waiting for me in the doorway. Kit wears a swim tank top and boy shorts, a sliver of her belly on display, and Evelyn wears a red vintage-inspired one-piece that ties around the neck and shows the roll on her upper back.

"Let's go, Maggie!" Kit yells. "The only thing that got me up and down that hill fourteen times today was the thought of belly flopping into that lake."

I pull my dad's old University of Texas T-shirt over my head and shoot to my feet armed with my sunscreen and red sunglasses.

"Have either of you ever ridden a Jet Ski before?" Evelyn asks. "I'm quite nervous."

"Nope, but I'm not letting that stop me," I tell her.

"I rode on a snowmobile behind my uncle once," Kit says.

I nod. "That's pretty close to the same thing I think. Right?"

As we break through the tree line near the docks, we run headfirst into a cluster of enraged campers in swimsuits. Trust me when I say there's nothing worse than angry kids in dry swimsuits on a hot day.

"This is false advertising!" someone yells.

"This doesn't make any sense!" another angry voice says.

On the other side of the dock, I hear sobbing, and then a very upset camper stomps through the crowd, pushing right through the three of us.

"Guys?" Kit says as our little tripod re-forms. She's a head taller than me and Evelyn, so when she jumps on her tiptoes for an even better vantage point, she can almost see over the crowd. "I think I know what the problem is."

The three of us link hands, snaking through the crowd, and suddenly we've made it to the action, where we've got a front-row view of Camp Sylvania counselors putting huge padlocks on the Jet Skis.

"It's simply a liability issue," William says in a much too delighted voice from where he sits in the lifeguard chair under an umbrella with his whistle dangling from his lips and blue sunscreen on his nose. "Only fifteen swimmers in the lake at once, by the way."

"What if we just want to use the blob?" someone asks.

Sloane grins as she paddles out to the blob in a canoe with a giant kitchen knife on the seat beside her. "Also off-limits."

When she reaches the blob, she holds the knife up above her head like she's starring in one of Dad's slasher stories.

Some kids cover their eyes while others burrow into their friends' shoulders.

Sloane cackles as she drives the knife down into the blob and it immediately begins to deflate.

I let out a gasp. That was just unnecessary. "She enjoyed that way too much," I whisper.

Evelyn and Kit nod in agreement.

William counts out fifteen lucky kids who quickly step away from the group to make it clear that they have been chosen. "All right, the rest of you go make yourselves busy. Make some crafts. Donate blood. And don't forget, auditions start at four o'clock today!"

Logan and Hudson are two of the lucky few and they sheepishly wave to us from the other side of the dock.

"This is ridiculous!" a voice behind me shouts.

I turn to see Charlotte there with Tori by her side.

"You know," Charlotte says, "a lot of you are new here, but it wasn't always like this. You can ask Captain B. She'll tell you."

"And what exactly will Captain B tell you?" Sylvia asks as she practically floats down the dock with an umbrella-carrying assistant. "Will she tell you about how this camp was about to go under? Will she tell you that if it weren't for me and my team, you'd all be at military camp or worse—wasting away in front of screens all summer?"

Charlotte's nostrils flare. "Maybe you don't want to help a bunch of chubby kids. Maybe you really need us all to go on your silly diet and do all your torturous exercises because you're scared of us! You're scared of looking like us again. And—and maybe you're taking away the Jet Skis and the blob because you don't think we deserve to have fun. Because to you, we're just a bunch of worthless *fat* kids."

Whoa.

I look around to see if everyone else just heard what I just heard, but everything and everyone is so still and quiet that even the birds have stopped chirping. The fish have stopped . . . making fish noises!

Tears run down Charlotte's cheeks, but they're not the sad kind. They're the angry kind.

Sylvia's eyes widen for a brief second, and I swear I can see flames in her pupils. Or maybe it's just the reflection of the red punctured blob being pulled to shore like a deflated parachute. Still, we're all bracing for the moment she opens her mouth and eviscerates Charlotte.

Then again, what's the worst they could do to us? It doesn't get much more awful than this, and I'm pretty sure any of us would line up to be sent home.

But then Sylvia blinks and her fiery expression is traded for a calm and serene one. "That's absurd. I *care* about you. I care about you all. Because I *was* you. And Jet Skis are the second-highest cause of accidental death. Now, wouldn't that be tragic," she says as she looks right at Charlotte, "if something happened to one of you."

A chill runs down my spine. Or maybe that's just sweat rolling down my back.

Sylvia turns to walk up the dock to her trailer as William walks back to his lifeguard stand, chuckling, and nudges one of the lucky fifteen kids on the shoulder, pushing them into the water.

"The rest of you!" Sloane calls. "Find another way to spend your free time!"

CHAPTER TEN

"What are we supposed to do now?" Kit asks as we wander the grounds.

The Blood Bank is full, and I'm not surprised since rumor has it they serve warm chocolate chip cookies.

"Well, there are auditions before dinner. Maybe we could watch those. I heard Tori say the disc golf course is overrun with poison ivy," Evelyn says as her feet shuffle across the dirt path. "And that Sylvia sold the go-karts."

Not only are Jet Skis off the menu, but the thought of running up and down this hill every day without the comfort of knowing I can float around in the lake all afternoon as a consolation prize is absolutely soul-crushing.

"Do y'all hear that?" I ask even though I barely hear anything myself.

They both give me an uncertain look, but follow closely behind as I walk toward the voices coming from the craft barn.

I step inside just in time to hear: "*Gruesome*, the most murderous podcast out there, is brought to you by Meal Box, your go-to meal in a box. Next week on *Gruesome*—"

"Are you listening to murder podcasts in a barn? By yourself?" I ask as I step into the dark, cool building to find Captain B whittling a piece of wood.

Captain B shoots to her feet and fumbles for the Bluetooth speaker to turn it off before we hear anything too bloody, I assume.

"It's okay," I tell her. "My mom is obsessed with *Gruesome*. She listens to it while she gardens."

Captain B sighs. "That sounds therapeutic, actually. Your mom sounds like my kind of people."

Evelyn steps forward and picks up a smooth, pointed piece of wood from the table. "What exactly are you making?"

Captain B holds up the piece she's working on. "Wooden stakes." And then she quickly adds, "For the musical set. It's going to make a fence."

Dropping her tools and digging into a little pouch hanging from her belt, Captain B scoops a handful of sunflower seeds into her mouth. "You three off to cool down in the lake for the afternoon?"

"Only fifteen kids in the lake at a time," I tell her morosely.

"And we didn't make the cut," Evelyn adds.

"I guess it makes sense with only one lifeguard . . . ," Kit says with failed optimism. "But we got our swimsuits on for nothing. And Maggie's even has cute bananas on it!"

"Bananas, huh?" Captain B asks. "Maggie Bananas. That's got a nice ring to it."

"The bananas are pretty cute." I shake my head. "They locked up the Jet Skis too. And deflated the blob! It's more like a bloop than a blob now."

Captain B grits her teeth, forcing a smile. "Well, you girls are welcome in the craft barn any time." She points to our feet. "But no flip-flops allowed."

"Safety first," Kit says firmly.

"I hope to see you three here for auditions later today," she says as she dives back into her work. "And if not, I could always use some stagehands."

As the three of us wander out into the muggy afternoon sun, Evelyn asks, "Where to now?"

The path in front of us breaks off into three directions: our cabins, the cafeteria, and—

"The computer lab," I tell them. "I saw a sign for a computer yesterday. It's time to send out an SOS."

"My dad's on a business trip to Japan, so it might be a few days before he can respond," Evelyn says.

Kit shrugs. "And there's no way I'm going home early and ruining my shot at Girl Scout camp and Space Camp next summer. Anyway, my family is big on two things: rules and commitments, which means I'm here for the long haul."

"Bribery. I guess it works, huh?" Truthfully, though, I've felt guilty all day thinking about leaving Evelyn and Kit behind. It's not even been a full day and already I feel like the three of us are bonded. But I have to tell them I want to go home, especially if I'm about to send an email telling my parents that I'm done.

"Listen, I like you two a lot," I tell them. "But I'm just not cut out for this place. And I'm pretty sure my parents would feel the same way if they knew what it was really like here. We've only been here for a day and already it feels like six."

"We haven't even donated blood yet," Kit says, like it's been on her bunkmates bonding bucket list and like it isn't totally bizarre for twelve-year-old kids to be giving blood without their parents' permission.

Neither of us bothers answering her, because after the worst twenty-four hours ever, all I can think about is getting into that computer lab—which is surely air-conditioned. It has to be, right? Don't computers overheat like the same way cars do or something?

As we approach the little shack at the end of the trail, I take off into a sprint, my flip-flops stirring up dirt with every step. I'm so close to this nightmare being over!

I'll do anything. I'll go to work with my mom every day. I'll feed our neighbors' parakeet while they're on vacation even if I'm terrified of it and its sharp beak. I'll watch the news all day if I have to! THE! NEWS!

I swing the door open, waiting for the cool, refreshing rush of air-conditioning to hit me, but all that I inhale when I take a deep breath is a whole mess of dust and maybe even a bug or two.

I cough into my elbow and when I open my eyes, all I see is one dusty old computer that looks more like a museum artifact than anything else.

"Oh, pants!" Evelyn says, and the way she says *pants* makes it sound like it could very well be a curse word.

"Pants?" I ask.

"It's a British thing, I think," Kit whispers. "I heard it on *The Great British Bake Off* when I visited my sister."

"Well, *pants* is right," I say.

Evelyn steps past me and over a spilled chair to get a better look at the one lone computer that is probably as old as the three of us put together. "Well, I daresay this thing has hosted more rodents than files recently."

"It won't even turn on?" I ask, trying to peer past the table, but unwilling to face the huge spiderweb that stands between us and the computer.

"The computer lab is closed," croaks a shadowy figure in the opposite corner.

The three of us scream for our lives and fumble for each other until we're just a pile of arms and legs.

Helen, the tiny counselor we met last night, steps forward so that we can just barely make out her features.

"Helen?" I ask.

"That's what's on my name tag," she says with a chuckle even though her expression is completely still, like she's a ventriloquist's dummy.

"We—we were just trying to email our parents. To—to

check in," I say, my voice practically shaking.

She laughs again, but this time it's more cruel. "Silly girls. It's camp! You don't need computers in the wilderness."

"But how are we supposed to talk to our parents?" Kit asks.

"Well, write them a letter, of course. There's a mailbox up by the offices." She takes a step closer to us, and her lips spread into a grin that is much too wide for someone as small as she is.

"Wonderful. I love old-fashioned stuff like that," Evelyn says too brightly as she tugs us both backward and out the door. "Thanks, Helen!"

My heart is beating so loud and hard that I'm sure other people can hear it.

The three of us trip backward through the doorframe.

"See you tonight, girls!" she says in a singsong voice. "Be sure not to miss your curfew. I'll be watching." Her voice is quiet but somehow carries as we race back to our bunk.

CHAPTER ELEVEN

William and Sloane sit side by side on the stage in directors' chairs.

After my failed attempt at writing an email to my parents, I decided to audition. I have plans to write a letter home ASAP, but I don't even know how long it takes for old-fashioned mail to be delivered, so I guess I might as well audition in the meantime.

"Welcome to auditions," Sloane says. "William and I are pleased to announce that the inaugural Camp Sylvania musical is—*The Music Man*!"

I've never seen that one, but the high school I'll be attending in a few years did it last spring.

William nods. "Because we are equal opportunity codirectors, casting decisions will be made without gender in mind."

Tori raises her hand. "So would we change the title to

The Music Wo-Man if a girl were cast for the lead role?"

"Oh, that's good," Sloane mutters as she scribbles it into her notepad.

"Yes," William agrees. "We are open to taking creative liberties."

Sloane stands. "But first, we need to see what we're working with."

"My expectations are in the basement," William says with a smile befitting a beauty queen.

I turn around to see Evelyn and Kit sitting in the back row with the rest of the kids who want to work tech for the show. They both give me a double thumbs-up and I try not to whimper. Behind them, Captain B sits at her desk in her office with the door ajar. She wears a headlamp as she continues to carve away.

"We'll ask each of you to come up onstage and perform a song of your choosing," Sloane tells us as she paces. "And because we want to hear your raw vocals, this will all be a cappella."

"And because we don't actually have any live instruments," William adds. "Or the ability to play them."

There are about twenty of us auditioning for the musical, and William and Sloane just start calling random names. It's total chaos! No alphabetical order or even the order we're sitting in, so there's no telling when I'll be up. My whole body tenses into a knot every time someone finishes their song, because my time could come at any moment.

When it's Charlotte's turn, she sings a belting Broadway-feeling song that I've never even heard of. Her voice is so big and sinks smooth and low before flying high.

I lean over to Logan, who looks more like himself in a black T-shirt with the word *meow* written in very tiny letters and black denim shorts that are frayed and full of holes. "Is it too late to back out?"

"I don't know what would be worse," he whispers. "Working with Sloane and William every day or the absolutely crushing look they'd give you if you snuck off now." His smile glows through the darkness of the barn.

"Oof. When you put it that way . . ."

"Maggie Hagen," William says. "You're up next."

"Go get 'em, Hagen," Logan says.

I take a deep breath and stand up. This is no big deal, I tell myself over and over again. You may not have your best friend and forever costar with you, and you might not really even know any of these people, but it feels like it would be near impossible for this summer to get any worse. The worst that could happen is that I don't make the cut and end up helping Captain B with the set.

The minute I found out we had to sing a song of our own choosing, I decided on "Shake It Off" by Taylor Swift. It's one of my mom's favorites and we've spent many car rides singing along with the windows rolled down. If there's any song I know by heart, it's this one.

But as I step onto the stage and stand under the lone spotlight, I freeze. My muscles. My brain. Everything. Just sing the song, I think to myself. You know this! It's burned into your brain!

William and Sloane sit in their chairs off to the side and I can see them looking back and forth between one another, grimacing.

"Whenever you're ready," Sloane says even though what she really means is *get this over with already.*

I open my mouth to sing. "I got—I have—" I take a breath. "I'm sorry. I'm just having like a mental brain freeze."

"Sing 'Happy Birthday'!" someone in the audience shouts. Maybe Logan?

I squint into the hazy darkness to just barely make out Logan with his hands cupped around his mouth. "You got this, Hagen!"

My stomach feels squishy and uncertain. But I also know that song. I know "Happy Birthday"! I clear my throat and begin to sing. "Happy birthday to you . . . Happy birthday to youuuuuuuu . . ."

I stare into a wooden post at the center of the barn and just concentrate on that until the song is either over or my body stops singing. When I'm done, I walk off the stage and past William, who whispers to Sloane, "I didn't even get to blow out any candles."

Sloane snickers, and I walk as fast as I can back to my spot next to Logan.

"You okay?" he asks.

"Yeah, thanks for the save. My brain went totally blank."

"It happens. A few weeks ago, I took a test and stared at the line next to where it said *Name* for a solid two minutes before remembering what I was supposed to write."

Covering my mouth, I stifle a laugh as the next camper is called up. "Okay, that's super relatable. I thought that just happened to me."

The auditions are all over the place, which makes me feel a little better. Even though it does make me feel bad to see other kids choke, it's nice to know I'm not alone. Tori and Charlotte are definitely the strongest. They're really good, and not just for camp. Like, actual real-world good.

"Isabella Gardener, you're up," Sloane says.

A white girl in front of us who I recognize from the bus ride here with perfectly curled auburn hair swept halfway back and wearing Sweat With Sylvia–branded leggings and a matching activewear top shoots to her feet. I'm not saying there's some magic number before you're fat enough to go to fat camp, but if there were, Isabella would definitely be toeing the line.

"Um, yes," she says. "I'll be singing 'Meet the Plastics' from *Mean Girls* the musical and my girlies from Cabin Six—or as we call ourselves, Sylvia's Sweeties—will be singing backup if that's all right."

Sloane and William whisper to each other for a moment, before William says, "We'll allow it."

Two girls on either side of Isabella—one white with a blond bob and the other with a medium brown complexion and braids—jump to their feet to join her.

Logan sways to the beat of their song, and they even have a little bit of choreography, which is so smooth and put together that I can't help but wonder if they knew each other before camp even started. The two other girls even do a little lift with Isabella where they hold her up by her arms.

Show-offs. I hate feeling jealous, but sometimes it just eats me up.

When the girls finish, they end with a pose, and people clap! They clap! Even Charlotte and Tori. The choreography was good and the song wasn't bad either, but I did notice a few times when Isabella was out of tune and even fumbled over a few words. Not that I have much room to talk after my birthday serenade.

Suddenly, I realize I'm the only holding back on the applause, so I join in. I might be a teeny bit jealous, but I'm definitely not going to let it show.

Logan is the last to go. He steps onto the stage and doesn't seem to be even a little bit uncomfortable.

Sloane nods at him and he bobs his head for a moment before singing the opening lines of "Adore You" by Harry Styles.

He floats around the stage effortlessly, and really sings to everyone. Not just Sloane and William.

For a brief moment, his eyes make contact with mine—or at least I think they do. I could barely see when I was up there, so who knows?

Something in my tummy flutters. I want him to stop singing so the feeling goes away, but also for him to never stop singing so that this feeling never ends.

Is this what crushing feels like? My ears feel hot. I'm not cut out for this.

As Mr. Phan, our choir teacher, would say, the boy has charisma.

"That was awesome," I whisper to him as he sits back down, but I'm all tongue-tied, so it actually comes out as "That was wowsome."

He grins. "Thanks. I get so embarrassed to sing in front of people, but it's a little easier here when you don't know anyone that well."

My shoulders slope with the tiniest bit of disappointment, because I want Logan to count me as someone who knows him well. But I don't think that's going to happen, especially if I get out of here as quickly as I hope.

"All right," William says as the stage lights come up fully. "We'll see you back here tomorrow for the dance audition. Practice those pirouettes and ball changes, people!"

That night, in my cabin, I write a letter to my parents by flashlight.

Dear Mom and Dad,

I miss you guys a lot and I think it's time I come home. I know it might be difficult to believe, but I've tried really hard to have a good attitude about this place. I even tried out for the musical! (Which I bombed, by the way!!!) And I regret to inform you that after being here for a whole twenty-four hours, I might not survive the next three weeks if you don't come and get me the moment you read this letter.

100% Serious and 0% Dramatic,
Maggie

Just as we're about to turn the lights out, there's a knock at the door.

I look to Evelyn and then Kit, who says, "Don't look at me. It's not like I'm expecting company."

Evelyn's gaze bounces from me to the door. "Who is it?"

For a long moment, the only noise is the cicadas chirping.

"Camp staff," a voice finally says.

Evelyn nods, so I step toward the door and open it, the hinges letting out a long creak.

Helen stands there, barely visible in the darkness. She steps forward into the light leaking out from our cabin. The toe of her hiking boot touches the doorframe and she practically jumps back, like she's been stung.

"I'm just doing an impromptu head count. Can't have

any campers out past their curfew," she says.

"Well, we're all here," Kit says.

Helen smirks as she slips back into the darkness. "All three in Cabin Three. One, two, three, one, two, three . . ."

I pull the door shut and latch our very inadequate lock.

"Talk about nightmare fuel," Kit mutters.

Evelyn and Kit get into bed, and I turn off the lights before dashing under my covers.

"I think I'm comfortable enough with you both to admit that I'm really, really starting to regret my decision not to bring a night-light," I tell them.

CHAPTER TWELVE

After a mostly sleepless night replaying my audition over and over again, and intermittent dreams of Helen standing outside of our bunk in the shadows as she counts over and over again, we wake up to three new rules.

Amendments to the Rules:

- Visiting the Blood Bank is a required activity and must be done at least four times a week.
- Just to make it official: Only fifteen campers in the lake at once.
- Mirrors are not allowed to be hung in cabins.

"Mirrors?" Evelyn asks as we both read over Kit's shoulder. "Maybe it's something to do with Sylvia's weight-loss process? Like, the end of camp is supposed to be some big surprise reveal for us when we finally look in the mirror."

"Or maybe it's because mirrors can cause glares and shine into other cabins?" Kit offers sensibly.

"Or maybe they're all vampires," Evelyn says with a laugh.

"Yeah, because vampires love camping." I snort. "Dad's vampires couldn't see their own reflection . . . but they also melted in the sun."

We spend the morning sweating until we're dizzy. Even though the mornings should be cooler, the air is so thick with humidity that my glasses fog immediately and all of us are sweating faster than we can drink Sylvia's patented red electrolyte sports mix.

I drop my letter for home in the camp mailbox after lunch and since we don't make it to the dock in time to swim during free time, I go with Kit and Evelyn to donate blood. I guess it can't hurt to do a little bit of good and maybe get a cookie for it before my parents hopefully rescue me in a few days.

"Are you sure you shouldn't get ready for your second audition today?" Evelyn asks.

I sigh. "I think it'd be best if I saved myself the humiliation and didn't go at all."

Kit sniffs into the air. "Does anyone else smell warm cookies?"

The Blood Bank is in a huge white trailer like the one that comes and parks outside of my mom's hospital sometimes for blood drives. On the side of the trailer is a giant cartoon drop of blood with an almost eerie smiley face, arms, and legs alongside the letters CBB.

Kit squints. "CBB?"

I take a few steps closer to read the small letters at the bottom. "Council Blood Bank."

"Well, I suppose we should get this over with," Evelyn says as she swings the door open.

I brace myself for the worst as I step inside. If my first full day at camp is any indication, this is going to feel more like a horror movie than a blood donation.

But I gasp as I'm greeted with a gust of deliciously cold, crisp air. "Is that . . . air-conditioning?"

"Welcome to the Blood Bank," says a warm, cheerful woman in white scrubs. "I'm Nurse Belinda, and I guess if this were an actual bank, I would be the banker." She laughs to herself. "But this isn't an actual bank, of course."

"Well, that would be weird," Kit says with a snort. "This is a stickup! Give me all your blood!"

That gets a hearty laugh out of Nurse Belinda.

Just behind her, I notice rows of plush white recliners with IV bags and medical equipment. On each recliner is a big fluffy blanket, huge headphones, and—oh my gosh—tablets! This is the camp oasis I've been searching for!

"Can we email on those?" I ask.

Nurse Belinda shakes her head. "Oh, heavens, no. Those are for streaming only."

"Right," I mutter under my breath. "Of course."

We each take a turn signing in and then Nurse Belinda leads us down the length of the trailer. "At the back are restrooms and a snack bar with cookies, juice, and just about anything else you can imagine."

"Did she say cookies *and* juice?" Evelyn whispers.

We'd heard about the cookies, but didn't think they could actually be real.

Nurse Belinda has us each sit back in a recliner and, despite the lack of email access, I truly cannot believe my luck.

Kit holds up the tablet and headphones. "Um, Nurse Belinda, I don't think we're allowed to have snacks like that—"

I shush her as discreetly as I can. "Really, Kit?"

She grimaces.

Nurse Belinda grins as she preps her tray of needles and supplies, and her eyes widen with excitement like she's setting a table for the most delicious meal. "We've got to keep that blood sugar up if you're donating. The tablets are contraband too, but girls, in my Blood Bank, the rules don't apply. At least not all of them . . ."

"Did you hear that, Kit?" I ask with a wolfish grin. "The rules do not apply."

I sink back into my chair and fluff the blanket up over my lap as I scroll through the catalog of movies and television shows. Now, this is the good life.

By the time it's my turn for Nurse Belinda to insert the needle into my arm, I don't feel a thing.

As I'm walking down the path to our cabin and past the craft barn, Logan stops me.

"Did you forget something in your cabin?" he asks.

"No." I shake my head.

"The audition's back this way," he says, nudging his head toward the barn.

I bite down on my bottom lip for a moment, before just admitting the truth. "I was sort of thinking of maybe just sticking to the tech crew for this one."

He shakes his head. "No way! Not uh! You were great yesterday!"

I roll my eyes. "I sang 'Happy Birthday.'"

"A great song!" he tells me. "So great that I sing it to all my favorite people!"

I kick at a pebble and dig the toe of my sneaker into the dirt. "I think I'm going home," I finally say. "I just wrote my parents asking them to come get me, so I'm pretty sure they'll be here any day."

The playful expression on his face shifts to something more serious. "You think the people who *sent* you to fat camp are just going to come and rescue you because you said you want to go home?"

I let out a loud *humph*. It's not that simple, and he obviously doesn't understand. I turn and begin to march back to my cabin. "And maybe watch your volume on the *F* word!"

"Wait, wait!" He chases after me and reaches for my shoulder. "I'm sorry. I really am."

I don't want to be annoyed with him, even if he probably

won't remember me by the end of the summer, but sometimes my feelings just bubble up inside of me until I can't ignore them. "It's fine," I tell him without stopping.

"Maggie, just wait!"

I stop and turn around with my arms crossed.

"I didn't mean to be rude. I'm sure your parents love you. A lot! I just think that . . . none of us really want to be here, you know?"

"I'm pretty sure Isabella wants to be here."

He rolls his eyes. "I think she might be the exception. I figure whoever sent each of us here wasn't really taking the time to listen beforehand, so why would they listen now?"

I'm silent for a little too long, because I get what he means, but I just can't see my parents ignoring a letter like that. The thought makes me want to curl up in bed with the sheets over my head and cry. "I just . . . can't handle being here."

"I hope they come and get you," he says with a kind smile. "I really do, but just in case you're stuck here for the next three weeks, why not finish the audition? Everyone would understand if you left partway through. And the dance part can't be that hard. Sloane and William are like skinny versions of Tweedledee and Tweedledum."

I snort. "Okay, fine. But if I fall, I'm going to say it's because you tripped me."

"Deal!" He beams like he's just won a bet.

And maybe he did.

I follow Logan back to the barn, and William and Sloane teach us a dance that feels like half musical theater and half music video. Let's just say, Sloane told us to, "Pop those boo-ties!" more than once. It feels totally ridiculous, but Logan keeps his promise and does every move right alongside me. And when I trip just a little, he's the first to say, "She tripped on my untied shoelaces! My bad!"

As I look around and watch everyone's attempts to fol-low along with the choreography, I'm surprised and a little bit pleased to see that Logan and I are definitely not the bot-tom of the barrel.

And hey, I'll take what I can get.

CHAPTER THIRTEEN

That night at dinner, Captain B announces that she's hosting a bonfire down by the lake, and it seems like the kind of camping rite of passage that I can't pass up.

"I've never been to a bonfire," Evelyn tells us as Logan and Hudson wave us over to their log.

I feel a bug land on my cheek and go to swat it away, but nearly smack myself in the face instead. Real smooth.

Logan and Hudson laugh, and I can't blame them, so I join in.

"The best part about bonfires is toasting marshmallows, and since that's not happening, the best we can hope for is that the bugs have mercy on our souls," I say, certain that another critter is crawling up my arm, but trying my best not to look like I'm possessed.

"The best part about fires is *starting* them," Kit says with a smile.

Both Evelyn and I pause and turn back to her.

"Should we be scared?" Evelyn asks.

"Just because I have an appreciation for fire starting doesn't mean I'm a pyromaniac," Kit says matter-of-factly.

Evelyn and I nod in unison.

"You're full of surprises, Kit," I tell her.

Kit grins. "Hey, if we're all ever stranded in a dark, damp forest, you're gonna be glad to have me with you."

As we sit down next to Logan and his brother, Captain B paces in front of the fire.

"I guess this is all of us," she says, looking around at the sparse crowd.

Hudson points up the hill. "I saw a bunch of kids lined up at the Blood Bank."

"I'd sleep in there if I could," I mumble.

"And I think a lot of people are still tired from today," he adds.

"I'm still tired from yesterday," Evelyn pipes in.

If the audition wasn't enough, William had us running up and down the hill again after an intense kickboxing session led by Sloane. One kid even overheated and another kid hit the punching bag so hard, it swung back and knocked her out cold. The nurse's office is becoming the second busiest place here. (Not Nurse Belinda, sadly. Just the normal nurse.)

"Well, I thought we could play some games or I could teach you a couple of old Camp New Beginnings songs, but I guess our group is a little too small for that," Captain B says.

"To be honest, I'm still having flashbacks of my audition gone wrong," I admit. "So I'm not really in the mood for singing."

"Well, maybe you can tell us about this place before Sylvia bought it," Kit says.

"Yeah, before they locked up the Jet Skis," Logan chimes in.

Captain B looks over her shoulder up the hill to see the swarm of campers waiting at the Blood Bank and the sound bath tent beside Sylvia's camper all lit up. She turns back to us. "So I actually started out at Camp New Beginnings when I was your age."

"Whoa," Hudson says. "Was that like back in the eighties?"

Captain B scoffs. "The year was 2001, thank you very much, and this place had already been in business for twenty-five years."

"Was it a fa—weight-loss camp back then too?" I ask.

"Technically, yes," Captain B says. "But not a very good one. Hank and Moira Holt, the original owners, were bigger people too, and sometimes I wondered if this place was supposed to be a haven for fat kids more than anything else. They weren't perfect, but they did the best they knew how."

"How did you end up working here?" Evelyn asks.

"Well, I started working as a junior counselor every summer in high school, and then in college too. Hank and Moira really needed someone to work as a caretaker during the off-season, so the summer after college I came back as a counselor and . . . I never really left."

"Is it true what they say?" I ask. "About the ghost on the docks?"

Captain B stands up to tend to the fire. "I'm pretty sure your parents aren't paying me to scare you to death."

"My dads don't have to pay anyone to scare me to death," Kit tells her. "My older sister does it for free."

Logan snorts. "That's a good one."

Hudson rolls his eyes. "I feel very seen right now."

"Please, Captain B. You gotta tell us," I beg. A camp ghost might just be the most exciting thing about this place.

"Isn't half the charm of coming to an American summer camp the spooky stories around the fire?" Evelyn asks.

That makes Captain B pause and sit back down. "I do wish you kids were getting the kind of camp experience I had—not that Sylvia and her program don't serve some sort of . . . purpose, I guess."

I nod excitedly. "Yes, take pity on us!"

Kit points to the red rash on the inside of her thighs. "If it'll make you feel any worse, running up and down that hill for the last few days has made the inside of my legs feel like someone took a cheese grater to them."

"Oh, jeez, kid," Captain B says as she sucks in a sharp breath. "I'm taking you to the nurse first thing in the morning. And don't feel bad. In a camp full of fa—bigger kids, you're not the only one battling some chafing issues."

I pat Kit on the back. I had the same problem last summer, and after my mom caught me walking around the house like I'd just ridden a horse halfway across the state, she handed me a stick of deodorant and told me to apply liberally to my sensitive skin. At the time, I was mortified, but being here with this group of people where I don't feel like such an outsider, it's nice to see everyone nodding along with Kit. We've all been there. I can't be the only person who stared at other girls in gym and wondered what it would feel like to live in a world where my thighs didn't touch. I make a mental note to share my secret remedy with Kit back at our cabin.

Captain B shrugs in defeat. "All right, all right. Against my better judgment, let me tell you about Camp New Beginnings' famous ghost: Howie Wowie."

"Wait. His last name was Wowie?" I ask. "This is already the least scary ghost story I've ever heard."

"No, no, just his camp name. Kind of like a nickname," she says.

"Like Maggie Bananas?" Kit asks. "Or Captain B?"

"Exactly like that," Captain B confirms before continuing on. "The story goes that Howie Wowie was a true daredevil. A real showman from what I've been told. He was known for doing tricks on the Jet Skis and even some pretty impressive go-karting."

"I can't believe we missed out on Jet Skis and go-karts," Logan says, the heartbreak in his voice impossible to miss.

Captain B laughs. "Would it kill you to know we had waterslides too?"

I clutch my chest like someone's just stabbed me, and keel over on my side.

"Okay," Captain B continues as Kit helps me up. "So Howie. It was the summer of 1993 and Howie was playing Truth or Dare. There are truth people in this world and there are dare people. Howie Wowie? He was a total dare person."

"A boy after my own heart," Kit says with a nod.

"Howie's dare was to sneak out after hours and jump a Jet Ski over the blob," Captain B explains, the light of the fire dancing across her face. "In the dark! So Howie waited until all the counselors went to bed and fired up a Jet Ski. Everything seemed to be going okay as he was gaining speed, but then Howie decided to really show off and ride backward on the Jet Ski. He missed the blob and lost control of the Jet Ski, which crashed into one of the docks. Howie went flying, bounced off the blob, and wasn't seen again until they found his body on the shores of Camp Rising Star."

Silence settles over our little circle. It's one thing to be scared of some ghost who might not even be real, but to think of Howie as a real person with friends and family and hopes and dreams makes me feel like there's something caught in my throat.

"He wasn't wearing a life vest?" Evelyn asks quietly.

Captain B shakes her head. "Now he haunts the lake, swimming back and forth from one shore to the other and—"

"Dragging campers to their deaths?" I ask, eyeing the lake with a newfound terror.

"There have been some mysterious incidents in the lake." Captain B leans in. "People feeling as though they're being pulled underwater or suddenly forgetting how to swim. Some even say they've met a boy wandering the camp at night asking if they'll go swimming with him."

Logan shakes his head. "Never trust a ghost."

Captain B stands up. "But always trust your counselor, and this counselor says it's nearly time for your curfew. Believe me when I say you don't want to get caught out of your cabin after curfew."

She begins to shoo us away.

As we stand, I turn to her, "Captain B? What cabin was Howie in?"

"Cabin Thirteen," she says.

"But there is not a thirteenth cabin," Kit chimes in. "At least not according to the map."

Captain B nods. "Cabin Thirteen is long gone."

Well, I guess that's a little bit of a relief. "Thanks for the ghost story—true or not," I tell her. "Can we help you put the fire out?"

"I'm just fine out here on my own." She looks out to the dark, rippling lake. "I've never been scared of things that go bump in the night."

CHAPTER FOURTEEN

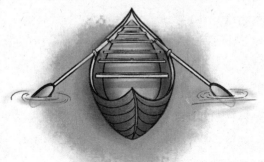

The moon reflects off the lake as I climb down the ladder into the water. Something splashes behind me, and I whip my head around to see, but the water is perfectly still.

I step down the next ladder rung, and something tickles my foot. Maybe it's just grass—or something. But it happens again and a loud shriek rips through me as I attempt to race back up to the dock, but whatever touched my foot has its grip on me and suddenly I'm being pulled down into the dark, murky water. I'm gasping and flailing as I try my best to fight back, but with every kick I'm pulled deeper until— I hear a scratching noise just behind my head. It stops and starts again a little louder this time.

"Mags," a voice whispers. "Maggie! Wake up!"

Turning over in my bed, I try to push away the nightmare of whatever is at the bottom of that lake.

"Maggie!" the voice says again.

I shoot up straight, my heart stammering in my chest.

"Maggie, back here!"

With my blanket clutched to me, I turn around despite every bone in my body begging me not to.

On the other side of my screen window is a shadowy silhouette that slowly leans in closer until—wait, I would know that French braid anywhere. And those braces!

"Nora?" We've been apart for less than a week and it somehow feels like months. "Are you real?" I ask, wondering for a moment if this is just another dream.

She laughs softly. "Uh, I'm pretty sure the bugs that ate me alive on my way over here agree that I'm real—and tasty. Are you going to leave me out here alone or what?"

"Oh, right!" I slip on my flip-flops and grab my flashlight from the windowsill. For a brief moment before I walk outside, I think about the curfew rules . . . but surely those don't apply if you need to go to the bathroom in the middle of the night or if there's an emergency. And I'm pretty sure my BFF appearing out of thin air outside my window counts as an emergency.

I hold the screen door carefully so that it closes slowly behind me instead of slamming shut. Checking for any sign of Helen first, I then race around the side of the cabin and run straight into Nora, our foreheads smacking together.

I throw my arms around her, ignoring the tiny knot forming on my head, and do my best to contain my squeals. "Nora! What are you doing here?"

She shrugs. "I missed you . . . and I thought you could use this." Reaching into her backpack, she pulls out a small package wrapped in foil. "I snagged an extra Fluffernutter from the cafeteria at lunch. I knew it was a sign to sneak over and check on you the moment I saw them being served."

I tear into the foil and nearly faint the moment I get a whiff of the perfectly combined salty peanut butter and whipped marshmallow. "I could get in so much trouble for this." I bite into the sandwich with a guttural moan. "Worth it."

We sit down on the ground behind a tree so that hopefully no one can see us from the path as I devour the delicacy she's brought me.

"How did you get over here?" I ask.

"A kayak. There's tons of them. And all other kinds of stuff to use on the lake." She rolls her eyes. "But everyone's so busy trying to show each other up onstage that no one even plays with all the cool stuff we have. I did sign up for a circus class that's inside of a big top. I figured whatever moves I learn, I could teach you when we get home."

My jaw drops. "Did you just say *big top*?" I thought I saw a red-and-white tent across the lake the other day, but I was starting to wonder if it was just a mirage.

"Yeah, it's this giant tent like they would have at those old-timey circuses. It's pretty cool. I got to use the trapeze. And tightrope too! Don't worry. They have a net for you to fall into."

I start in on the second half of my sandwich after demolishing the first half. "This place might as well be a prison."

"Yeah, it looks pretty rough," she confirms. "I noticed they deflated the blob."

"You can see us from over there?"

"I packed my binoculars. I look for you every day, but it's sort of hard to pick you out since everyone's wearing the same thing."

"They don't even have us doing fun exercise stuff like swimming or dancing or roller-skating. It's just mind-numbing. The best part of my day is visiting the Blood Bank."

"The *Blood* Bank?" she asks in total disgust.

I nod and tell her all about my oasis here at camp.

"Don't you have to be seventeen to donate blood?" she asks.

"I think that's for R-rated movies." I glance up the hill to where the craft barn sits. "We are doing a summer musical, though."

Her deep brown eyes widen. "I'm sorry, but did you just say *musical*?"

"Yep. *The Music Man* to be exact. Though the counselors directing it said they're not opposed to making it *The Music Wo-Man*."

"Whoa." She's awestruck. "Your counselors sound so cool."

I let out a ridiculous snort. "Trust me. That's the one and only cool thing about them. It's so weird . . . It's like if I saw them online or on TV, I'd probably think they were really cool, but in person they're just . . . mean and kind of desperate for attention."

"Popular kid syndrome," she confirms. "So did you audition?"

I sigh. "Unfortunately, yes." I relate the whole awful story to her and my embarrassment is validated when she cringes at the birthday song part.

"I bet you were still great," she says. "It doesn't matter what you sang as long as they got to hear you. And it sounds like you really nailed the dance audition. Besides, how many people even auditioned? I bet everyone gets a role or maybe even two. Camp Rising Star is doing *Les Mis Jr.* and I was cast as a dead body. There are so many campers and all of them are basically amazing. I'm honestly lucky I even got a part, but Mags, you could actually get one of the lead roles!"

"That's the last thing I want! You know what happens to me when I'm flying solo onstage." I shrug with my whole body, like I'm trying to prove to even myself that I don't care. "It doesn't matter, though. I wrote a letter home to my parents and I'm getting out of this place ASAP."

"Do you really think they'll come and get you?" she asks.

I grimace a little. Why does everyone keep saying that? I want to be mad that she would even think that, but I was already upset at Logan and it's hard to be angry at Nora when she knows me and my parents so well.

"Mags. I know you and I know that you are meant for stardom. You're the funniest person I know, and when you really let yourself belt it out, your voice is a powerhouse. And you can dance! You're a triple threat, Magpie. Maybe out here at this camp is your chance to turn a new leaf. A clean slate! Out here no one knows about *Annie* or even how nervous you let yourself get."

I want to believe her. I really do. But no matter how hard I try, I can't seem to see what my best friend sees in me. "Yeah, I guess I'd just be happy with getting onstage and not totally bombing. I don't think I can last long enough at this place to see this thing through, though. I haven't even told you about how creepy this place is. . . ."

Wings flap above our heads, and I instinctively crouch, but Nora doesn't seem to be bothered. Maybe this place is making me batty.

"I get it. I'm pretty freaked out being in the middle of nowhere too . . . but Maggie, you should really go for this musical. I've got a good feeling about this. Plus—"

A far-off scream pierces the air and I pull Nora to me. "Did you hear that?" I ask as quietly as I can.

She laughs nervously. "Probably just some older teenagers sneaking around . . . right?"

Another scream echoes down the hill, and this one sounds like more than fun and games.

Just then a flicker of light skips over the path, probably a flashlight somewhere up the hill shining down. It could be another camper . . . or Helen . . . or something else entirely . . .

"I better get back before someone catches me and makes me wear one of those awful uniforms," Nora says, trying to joke even though I can tell she's freaked out too. "What's that?" she asks in a whisper, pointing up the hill to Sylvia's giant Lotus tent, which is fully illuminated.

"Sylvia's sound bath," I tell her. "Don't even ask me what that means."

Up the path, we can hear the sound of feet shuffling and something . . . dragging . . .

I give her a hug, and hand her the foil wrapper since I can't be caught with any evidence of contraband. "You better go. I don't want you to get in trouble."

More lights flicker, but this time, the source of the light is narrower like it's getting closer.

"Be careful on that lake," I whisper as she tiptoes around the back side of the cabin.

"I will," she promises. "Some kid helped me pull my kayak in." She smirks. "He said the same thing."

"Wait. What?" I go to follow her around the corner, but the shuffling footsteps grow louder and closer.

"Did you hear that?" a voice asks.

I sprint to the front of the cabin.

"Hear what?" another voice asks.

"I heard it," another voice hisses.

I swing the door open and pull it shut as quietly and as quickly as I can before vaulting myself into bed.

The footsteps stop just outside the door of our cabin.

My stomach drops. Nora! I hope she's halfway across the lake by now. I wish there was some way I could warn her—a bat signal or something.

"Thump, thump, thump, thump," the third person, who

sounds like Helen's eerily, even-toned voice, says. "Thump, thump, thump, thump."

Her words are perfectly timed with the chaotic beating of my heart.

I hold my breath and squeeze my eyes shut. From outside, a flashlight passes in front of the screen window and over our three bodies tucked into our beds.

"Cabin Three. One, two, three."

"Come on," one of the voices says. "Let's go see if our visitors are enjoying their feast."

After a moment, my heart finally begins to slow as the sound of their footsteps grows farther and farther away.

So much is swirling through my brain as I try to fall back asleep, and the one thing that calms me enough to finally relax is the memory of hugging Nora.

I know you and I know that you are meant for stardom.

I don't know what Nora sees in me that I can't see myself, but one thing about my best friend is that she never says anything she doesn't mean.

When I finally drift off, it's with a new sense of determination. I'm going to do this musical. I'm going to make Nora proud and show Sylvia and my parents and all the kids back home that I am destined for greatness. No matter how I get there and even if it only starts with the chorus line.

Every rising star has to start somewhere.

CHAPTER FIFTEEN

"Maggie, come on, we can't be late," Kit says as she rips my blankets off me. "Plus the cast list should be posted outside the barn."

I roll over to escape her, only to find Evelyn sitting on the edge of her bed with a hunched back and deep circles under her eyes. She tosses my uniform at me. "Come on. Let's get this over with."

"Are you okay?" I ask. She doesn't look like herself at all.

She closes her eyes and inhales through her nose before nodding her head. "Just bad dreams. I'll feel better after I eat."

"Unlikely with that cafeteria selection," Kit mutters.

She's not wrong. Last night we ate liver and red onions on a bed of shredded cabbage.

Sluggishly, I shimmy into my uniform with a half yawn, half shriek. "Okay, let's go."

Kit holds up a piece of paper as I tie my shoes. "They're

changing the curfew! All campers must be in their bunks after sundown."

"I guess this means our first bonfire was our last," Evelyn says. "Maybe it's just as well."

I squint at the newly listed rule on the page. Why would they do that? Surely no one saw me last night. "That stinks," I finally say, remembering the screams and voices I heard last night. "I wonder why."

"I guess it doesn't really matter. You're out of here as soon as your parents get that letter," Evelyn says as we step out onto the path.

I puff out a heavy sigh. "Actually, I wouldn't be so sure. . . . I might just stick around."

"Well, that's a change in attitude," Kit grumbles not so quietly.

"I'll say," Evelyn agrees. "How can we be sure you weren't abducted by aliens and replaced with an alternate-reality version of yourself?"

"That would make a pretty good story, ya know." My mouth curves into a small smirk. "Plus . . . I guess I sort of like hanging out with you two."

Kit throws her arms around me in a bear hug and she pulls Evelyn along with her.

"She likes us!" Kit crows. "I love a good mushy moment!"

"This is a lot of hugging before breakfast," Evelyn says, her voice beginning to warm. "But I suppose it is nice."

After our hugging sesh, we trudge up the hill, and on our

way, we pass Cabin Twelve, where a counselor stands in the doorway, sweeping, and another is rolling suitcases out onto the path.

I peer past them to see beds that have been stripped of blankets and sheets. There isn't a single thing in place. "Isn't that Charlotte and Tori's cabin?"

Kit stops. "Maybe they got moved because of a bug infestation or something."

"We're in the woods," I tell her. "We're already infested."

"Right you are," Evelyn agrees.

As we turn the corner, we find a crowd of campers gathering around the doors of the craft barn.

"It's up!" Kit screeches.

I shed any sense of cool and push through the crowd to see what fate awaits me, but before I can reach the cast list, Logan steps in front of me.

"We're understudies!" he says in thrilled disbelief.

"What?" Excitement combined with a familiar sense of dread eats away at me. "For who?"

He has zero chill. "For the leads! The Music Man and Marian! Me for Marian and you for The Music Man."

"I—what? Me? The Music Man?" My jaw hits the floor.

"Well, actually the Music Wo-Man," he corrects. "Charlotte is playing that role and Tori is Marian."

This is not what I had in mind. I thought maybe I'd get a part with a few lines or a song even . . . but the understudies for the leads . . . well, my track record isn't so good. "I mean, it's just one night though. Surely they won't actually need us to step in, right?"

He nods. "Probably not, but it's still so exciting! We're in the chorus and if anything happens to Tori or Charlotte . . . obviously, I hope not. But if it did—showtime, baby!"

Just then Sloane and William push through the crowd. "Excuse us, excuse us," they say.

The campers divide for them, in awe of the power our snooty directors wield.

"Change of plans," Sloane says.

I trail close behind them, and Logan and I watch over their shoulders as William uses a black marker to draw sharp lines through Tori's and Charlotte's names.

The Music Wo-Man/Professor Harriet Hill . . .
~~Charlotte B.~~ *Maggie H.*
~~Marian~~ *Mario* . . . ~~Tori G.~~ *Logan N.*

Behind me someone gasps.

I try to speak, but nothing comes out. "Sh-shouldn't Logan at least play the Music Man?"

William laughs haughtily. "Let's just say that the human biology of puberty really works in the favor of gender-swapped casting."

Logan's cheeks flare with blush, but that doesn't stop him from asking, "What—what happened to Charlotte and Tori?"

"Not that it's any of your business," Sloane says. "But they were sent home."

William and Sloane step out of the way, and everyone else immediately swarms the updated cast list.

"For what?" I ask. "Why did they go home?"

William rolls his eyes. "Did you not hear the part about this being none of your business?"

"Practice starts today," Sloane reminds us. "Don't be late." She and William, with his awful whistle around his neck, leave us in their dust as they head off to the cafeteria.

"Maybe that's how you could get out of here," Evelyn whispers to me. "Just say the *F* word that everyone's thinking but no one is allowed to say."

Fat. She's right. The word *fat* is basically like our own little grenade. After the showdown on the docks between Sylvia, Charlotte, and Tori, I shouldn't be surprised, but it's hard not to feel like this isn't some kind of mistake or that I'm winning because someone else lost.

"I'm not going anywhere," I tell Evelyn. "For now, at least. I'm the Music Wo-Man. But it's always good to have a nuclear option. . . ."

During lunch, I write my parents a brand-spanking-new letter. They can't rescue me now. Not when things are just starting to get good.

Dear Mom and Dad,
I miss y'all and Pickle too. Especially Pickle,
actually. Give him some belly rubs for me.

I know my last letter home sounded a little intense. But you can't blame me! I was feeling pretty low. Adjusting to life here hasn't been easy, especially without Nora. But I wanted you both to know that I don't need you to rescue me. I didn't think I could make it until the end of camp, but I might just prove myself wrong.

I've made friends with my bunkmates, Kit and Evelyn, and not only am I in the camp musical—I'M THE STAR!

I can't wait to see you guys on Parents' Day. Don't forget to bring roses for my curtain call!

Love Your Favorite (and only) Daughter/Star of the Show/Pickle's Mother,
Maggie

WEEK TWO OF CAMP

CHAPTER SIXTEEN

"How is it this hot here?" Evelyn asks as the three of us rifle through our things, searching for our swimsuits.

"If you think this is hot, you should visit me back home in Texas," I tell her. "Some days it's so hot that pools feel like hot tubs."

Running back to our cabins to change into swimsuits and hopefully be among the lucky fifteen who get to swim has turned into a daily, camp-wide competition—one we have yet to win.

But today is the hottest it's been since we got here, and I'm riding the high of two straight days of musical rehearsals without William telling me I dance like a dying fish, so today, I am determined. And today that determination means cannon-balling into the lake that's been teasing me since we got here.

The three of us change into our swimsuits in a flash and the only thing that makes me pause for a second to put on my flip-flops is the fact that the grass that stretches along the lake is basically a public restroom for geese every morning. It's not pretty. Especially without shoes.

As we race down the path, I notice Isabella from Cabin Six and her two other Sylvia's Sweeties cohorts are making a beeline for the dock. Since the audition I've learned that Adelaide is the one with the bob and Nicolette is the one with the braids.

"Oh no they don't!" Kit says as she breaks off into a sprint.

"My legs are jelly!" Evelyn whines.

I take her hand and pull her with me to catch up with Kit. "And they'll be hot melted jelly if we don't make it into that lake."

As I'm running, I glance down and notice my bare, jiggling tummy and freeze. "Shoot!"

"What's wrong?" Evelyn asks. "If we stop for too long, I don't think I'll be able to start again."

"I'm getting in that water if it's the last thing I do!" Kit yells from up ahead.

"I forgot my T-shirt back at the cabin," I tell Evelyn. "I can't—I can't just go swimming like this."

Evelyn throws her arms out. "Maggie! Maggie Bananas! Look around. We're all going swimming like this!"

I look down at my tummy and then out at the sparkling lake.

This time it's Evelyn dragging me along. "Come on! We can't let Cabin Six take our spot."

I nod and we're off again, closing in on the dock.

Evelyn makes it there first, practically running into the kid in front of her. She does a quick head count before calling back to us. "Two spots left!"

Alongside us, Isabella and Adelaide leave Nicolette, who is a little too careful with each downhill step, in the dust.

That's the final push I need to run even faster. So fast I forget about what my stomach looks like and the fact that everyone can see me in my bananas bikini—a swimsuit I never thought would do anything other than live under soggy T-shirts.

We just barely cut in front of Isabella and Adelaide and slide into place next to Kit.

I brace my hands on my thighs, enjoying the victory, as I catch my breath.

William blows his whistle from where he sits on his life-guard chair. "Fourteen and fifteen. Have fun. Don't drown. Especially you, fifteen," he says as he points to me. "We don't have any more understudies left at this point."

The three of us squeal with delight under the beating hot sun and Isabella sticks her tongue out at us.

"Childish," Evelyn tells her with her fists planted on her hips.

"Let her pout," I say.

I kick off my flip-flops and we all join hands at the edge of the dock.

This camp is a lot of things. A lot of really crummy things. But one thing I didn't expect it to be is a place where

I can fit right in. A place where I'm not the only fat kid. A place where we're all the fat kid. A place where I can cannonball in my bikini without my T-shirt on and not feel like the world is going to end.

"On the count of three," I say.

Evelyn grins.

Kit counts us off. "One . . . two . . . three!"

The water is an instant relief, and once I'm below the surface, I open my eyes to find grass and the occasional shadow of a fish. Thankfully, there's not a single watery ghost hiding there in the lake grass, waiting to pull us under. At least that I can see . . .

After the lake, we take ice-cold showers before rehearsal that feel so good, especially since I forgot to put on sunscreen.

I forget my toiletries, so Kit shares hers with me, passing them over the concrete barrier dividing our showers.

"You know," Kit says, "all those fish in the lake got me thinking . . . What do you call a fish wearing a bow tie?"

"Hmmm," I say as I scrub her rose-scented shampoo into my hair.

"A formal lunch?" Evelyn says with a laugh.

"Okay, that might be better than the actual answer," Kit admits.

"Well, don't leave us hanging," I say.

Kit slaps her hands against the concrete for a drumroll: "So-fish-sticated!"

Evelyn snorts. "I love Dad jokes."

I rinse the shampoo from my hair before starting in on the conditioner, and slowly begin to hum "The Wells Fargo Wagon" song that I'd just learned in rehearsal the other day.

After a minute, Evelyn and Kit join in too, and soon we're singing at the top of our lungs. And when that song is over, Kit starts to sing the King George song from *Hamilton*, which is by far my favorite track, and I think this is what my mom meant when she told me how special her time at camp was.

We arrive early to rehearsal with arms linked as we fan our legs out like we're walking down the yellow brick road from *The Wizard of Oz*.

Captain B has pushed aside the set pieces and costumes in progress so that campers can come in and do a craft throughout the afternoon. "Well, don't you girls look like you're settling into life at camp," she says, smiling from behind her desk.

"We'd be adjusting even better if we could have another after-dark bonfire with you," I tell her.

"The new curfew is a little extreme, and I say this as someone who is very serious about the dangers of nature," Kit says. "Is Sylvia scared we're going to turn into werewolves or something?"

Captain B leans back in her chair and crosses her arms. "Actually, the curfew was my idea."

"What? Why?" I cross my arms over my chest, suddenly irritated with her.

"It's easy to forget that we're pretty much in the wilderness out here," she says.

"The wilderness?" I press. "I would hardly call this place the wilderness."

"Trust me. We get all sorts of wild animals around here, and they're most active at night." Her voice is full of mystery, and not the kind I have any desire to explore. If I didn't know any better, I might say it sounds like Captain B is threatening us. "But you girls don't need to worry about that, because you have a sundown curfew, right?"

"Riiiiiiight," we slowly agree.

She stands, and pushes the creases out of her khaki shorts. "Now, you girls haven't come to a single craft session since rehearsals began."

"You noticed?" Evelyn asks sheepishly.

Captain B snorts. "Pretty hard to miss you three. So since you're here early, how about you give today's craft a go?"

"Sure!" Kit sits down at a picnic bench that serves as one of the craft tables. "What are we making?"

"Walking sticks," Captain B says as she pulls three tall sticks from a barrel.

"Walking sticks?" Evelyn asks. "Aren't those the sort of thing that doesn't require any additional assembly?"

Captain B's brows raise. "Well, if you're boring, and if you are, just say so. But every avid outdoors person knows that a walking stick is just a stick until you add a little personal flair."

"She's right," Kit confirms. "My walking stick at home is painted hot pink and has charms hanging off the top."

"Nice." Captain B nods. "You can decorate them with yarn and badges. Because I'm pragmatic, I like to keep the end sharp just in case I run into a bear . . . or something. Now, who's ready to get started?"

I reach for neon-turquoise glitter paint, pink leather straps, and a bag of feathers. "Personal flair, huh?"

If I'm going to decorate a stick, I might as well make it fabulous.

CHAPTER SEVENTEEN

Okay, so here's the thing: I actually had no clue what *The Music Man* was about when I auditioned, and I definitely did not expect to accidentally get cast in the lead role. It's just one of those old musicals you always hear about, but never really know much about until you're actually doing it—or happen to see it. Like *Cats*! And honestly, even after my parents took me to see that one, I still don't think I actually know what it's about.

On the first day of rehearsals when William passed out our scripts, he gave us old binders full of photocopied versions of the original script with tons of stuff slashed through and entire chunks missing. "We'll be performing the abbreviated version," he explained and then mumbled something about copyrights.

Since we don't have access to the internet, I can only say what the show is sort of about based on our butchered script. Professor Harold (or Harriet in my case) Hill, played by me, is a con artist who is pretending to be a marching band organizer who travels from town to town teaching kids about music and organizing them into bands. (I guess that used to be a thing back in the day.) The professor's big plan is to sell uniforms and instruments to the kids and then cut out of town without giving music lessons *or* forming a band, but then everything changes when Marian the Librarian (now Mario the Librarian played by Logan) catches the professor's eye.

I read that part late at night and felt a deep and sudden embarrassment. I quickly skimmed to the end of the script and was relieved to find that the big kiss at the end had been crossed out with a big X in favor of a hug. (Which honestly still made my stomach feel like goo.)

Since then, I'd spent way too many hours of my day thinking about hugging Logan onstage. In front of the entire camp and all of our parents.

Today, we are finally getting to the point of the big hug in the script, which means last night I barely slept.

Deep breaths. Deep breaths.

I sit by Logan on the floor in front of the stage while the chorus stumbles through a dance number.

HUG. It stares back at me from my binder in huge letters. It's not like I've never hugged anyone who I wasn't related to.

"Hey," Logan says, nudging me with his elbow. "Are you okay? You look like you just found out how they make hot dogs."

I gasp a little, startled out of my spiral of HUG anxiety. "How *do* they make hot dogs?"

He holds his chin for a moment. "You know, I don't

actually know. I guess I just always heard adults talk about it being gross, but I really like hot dogs."

"Have you ever had a Korean hot dog, though?" I ask.

He leans in close. "You're telling me there are different kinds of hot dogs?"

"Oh yeah," I tell him. "Back home, we have a huge Asian shopping center with all kinds of stores and restaurants that you wouldn't even believe. The hot dog stand makes these things that are like corn dogs, but better, and you can even get cheese in them or all kinds of toppings. My best friend, Nora, gets hers rolled in Hot Cheeto dust."

His eyes are practically heart shaped. "Whoa. I gotta try one of those."

Hudson plops down in front of us, holding his belly. "Did someone say Hot Cheetos? Those are almost red. Shouldn't they be part of the Scarlet Diet?"

Logan points over to the group of kids at the back of the barn painting set pieces. "Don't you have a job to do?"

I look from Logan to Hudson, and I almost think that Logan might be wishing Hudson would leave us alone. Which would mean . . . Logan likes being alone—with me!

Hudson holds his hand up. "Splinters."

"Shouldn't you go to the nurse for that?" Logan asks.

And I have to admit, that's pretty logical.

Hudson throws his arms up. "Is it too much to want to hang with my big bro?"

"No," Logan says. "But we've basically been conjoined at

the hip for the last week."

"Which is how I know you fart in your sleep," Hudson tells him.

Logan pushes up from the floor and charges toward Hudson, but Hudson is off in a flash and runs out the barn doors.

He comes to sit back down with me. "Little brothers, ugh. If they're not driving you up a wall, you're saving their butt."

"Saving their butt, huh?"

"Oh, it never ends," Logan says. "The other day after lunch, he got the wise idea to sneak into Sylvia's trailer."

"What?" I whisper through a gasp. "That is totally off-limits . . . but I mean, what was in there?"

"Just a bed," he says with a shrug. "And like super-fancy furniture and a kitchen without any food. Just a fridge stocked full of her red smoothies. He said there was a bag of potting soil under her bed. I guess she's into gardening."

"Maybe?"

"Oh, he did say she has this huge sign over her bed that says LIVE, LAUGH, LOVE, but the LOVE part is scratched out and instead says NEVER MAKE A PROMISE YOU CAN'T KEEP."

I chortle. "Live, laugh, never make a promise you can't keep? That's actually not bad advice. My mom has one over the kitchen table that just says Gather. Like, what else are we going to do at the kitchen table?"

"Adults and their signs," he says, shaking his head.

"Harriet, Mario, you're up!" Evelyn says from her desk by

the stage with her homemade placard reading STAGE MAN-AGER, a role she was assigned today and one I think she was always destined for.

"Sorry about Hudson. He's mostly cool," Logan says. "For a little brother. But sometimes—"

"It's okay," I tell him as we step onstage.

"Are you okay though?" he asks again. "Before . . . you looked like . . . well, the hot dog thing."

I smile, my cheeks growing warm. "Right. I'm okay. Just . . . nervous about . . ."

"The hug?" he asks softly.

I nod. "Yeah, and everything else. It's a lot of pressure." Even though, mostly, it's the hug.

"We could just do like a fist bump until the night of the show. Actors do things like that all the time when they have to kiss and stuff. . . . It's not that I'm not okay hugging you or anything, but—"

"A fist bump," I say, the warmth in my cheeks spreading to my neck. "That sounds good."

He holds his fist up and I tap my knuckles against his.

That wasn't so bad, I tell myself as I try my best to ignore the spark that lit in my tummy the moment his skin touched mine.

This is fine. This is no big deal. Remember my lines. Don't flub the dance moves or forget the lyrics to the songs. And don't make googly eyes at my costar. No biggie.

I can do this.

I hope.

CHAPTER EIGHTEEN

Nurse Belinda waves us off after a successful trip to the Blood Bank, and we head out with our walking sticks in tow.

After being in the comfort of the air-conditioning, the humid air hits me in the face like a brick wall. "It sort of feels nice to do a good thing like donating blood . . . in air-conditioning, ya know?"

Kit's head rolls back and then down in a slow circle. "I can't decide if going in and out of the Blood Bank makes the heat better or worse."

We didn't get lucky enough to go swimming two days in a row, but I did spend my free time with Logan running lines while Kit and Hudson worked on the set and costumes, and Evelyn color coded her lighting cues. With all the extra work that has come with playing one of the leads, it does make the time go quicker. Sometimes.

If it weren't for the morning workouts and weigh-ins

from hell and the most bizarre cafeteria menu ever, I would say this place is almost starting to feel like a normal camp.

As we head down the path toward the cafeteria, Kit spins her walking stick around like it's a lightsaber. "I kind of like this thing. It makes me feel powerful."

"Well, maybe that's because you wrote KIT'S BIG STICK along the side in glitter paint pen," I say.

She makes the lightsaber sounds to go along with her movements now. "I wanted to assert my dominance," she tells us just as she accidentally flings the stick through the air like a javelin. "Oh no!" She covers her eyes as if that will make anything better.

The walking stick lands in the ground with a thud just inches in front of Sylvia.

Evelyn and I gasp.

The look on Sylvia's face is stern as her nostrils flare. It's enough to make all three of us cower.

"Sorry!" Kit calls as she runs over to retrieve her flying walking stick.

Sylvia pulls the stick out of the dirt like it's nothing. She holds the stick with two hands and then, without warning, snaps it like a twig.

"Holy schnikes," I say under my breath.

Evelyn lets out a low whistle.

"It was just a walking stick," Kit says in a small voice.

I run up alongside Kit. "And totally worth snapping, Sylvia—ma'am—Your Honor."

Sylvia drops the two pieces of walking stick on the ground. "Weapons will not be tolerated at Camp Sylvania," she says, and then walks into her trailer with her assistant and Steve the cameraman close behind.

"'Your Honor?'" Evelyn asks as soon as Sylvia's door closes.

I shrug. "It was the best I could do! She looked like she was about to snap Kit in half next."

"It was just a walking stick," Kit says again, sounding lost and confused.

First thing the next morning, there's a knock at our door.

"Did someone order room service?" I ask. "I'm coming, I'm coming," I call to whoever is on the other side of the door.

Evelyn and Kit are only just now waking up.

Evelyn yawns. "Ugh, now all I want is a big English breakfast."

"That sounds so good," Kit says through a groan. "And I'm not even grossed out about the beans on toast."

"Beans on toast?" I ask. "Why would anyone do that to themselves?"

Three more knocks bang against the door.

"Okay, okay. Coming!" I stand up and shuffle over.

Logan is standing there, his eyes watery and swollen. "Have you seen him?" he asks frantically through sniffles.

"Whoa, whoa, Logan, are you okay?" My whole body immediately wakes up as I quickly glance around to see if anyone is watching before I pull him into our cabin. No one said anything about boys and girls in the same cabins being against the rules, but I'm not taking any chances.

As I close the door, I see a new set of rules taped to our door. Great.

Logan is so upset that I don't even take a moment to feel awkward about him seeing me in my pajamas or seeing how messy our cabin is. I lead him to the edge of my unmade bed, and force him to sit down.

Evelyn puts on her slippers and sits beside him while Kit locks the absolutely pointless latch on our door.

"I just woke up in the middle of the night and he was— he was gone," Logan says.

"Who?" Evelyn asks.

But he doesn't have to say. I already know in my gut. "Do you mean Hudson?"

Logan hiccups. "I was in bed, and he left to go to the bathroom. When he came back, he tried to wake me up, but I was too tired. Maybe it was something about the splinters in his hand . . . I don't know. I woke up again a few hours later with a bad feeling and he was gone. I just thought he went back to the bathroom and fell asleep again."

Immediately, my stomach tangles into a knot. That doesn't sound like Hudson. Not that I know him very well, but I can't imagine him just leaving without talking to Logan first. "Did you try to find any counselors?" I ask.

"I went up to the main office just before sunrise and

133

Helen was there . . . She said Hudson asked to go home and that they'd already sent him to the airport. But he wouldn't just go—he wouldn't just leave me like that."

"He didn't leave anything?" Kit asks. "A note? Something?"

Logan covers his eyes as tears begin to stream down his cheeks. "I asked to call home, but they said the phone lines around here are down because of construction. Honestly, Hudson's scared of the dark. He'd kill me if he knew I was telling you all that, but I'm surprised he even went to the bathroom without me. Something about this isn't right."

It's hard to imagine a kid like Hudson who could probably hack his way into the CIA if he tried hard enough being scared of the dark, but I guess we all have fears of our own to battle.

I pat Logan's shoulder. He's right. Something is off, and I hate seeing him so upset. It makes me angry—the kind of anger that forces you to do something about it.

"We're going to figure this out," I promise him.

After a moment, the morning alarm sounds over the speakers, letting us know that it's time to get up and go to our first session before breakfast.

Logan nods and then heads back to his cabin to get changed for our morning activity.

As I watch him go, Kit reads over the new rule from the paper stuck to our door.

"No walking sticks," she says with a frown.

It's not that I don't believe Logan, but I'm still so surprised to find Hudson missing at every meal and every activity. If he's gone, who else is going to bite into a juicy beet and let it run down his face like blood? Or who else is going to pretend the steaks are cooked so rare that they're still mooing? Even though I know better, I expect him to be hanging out on the dock or over by the kickball field or even in the craft barn. But he's just nowhere to be found. Like he vanished into thin air.

That night after dinner, we walk Logan to his cabin. He hasn't been himself all day and barely kept up at rehearsal. After saying good night, we take the path down to our place.

Evelyn shakes her head, confused. "You know, back during week one, I heard some kid named Brooklyn just left out of nowhere. She was in Cabin Nine, but I didn't really think much of it because leaving was pretty much all any of us could talk about back then."

"Two kids from Cabin Seven went home the other day, and one of them even liked the food here." Kit makes a gagging noise.

I cringe at that. "That's weird, but kids go home from camp all the time," I say as we step into our cabin to get our toiletries. "Honestly, I call my parents to pick me up from slumber parties sometimes. Plenty of kids do. And I think we all agree that Charlotte and Tori were probably kicked out for breaking the rules. Or . . . maybe it's just aliens. My dad's first book was about a true crime podcaster who was investigating a missing person cold case, but it ends up being aliens."

Evelyn shrugs. "I don't know if I believe in little green men from Mars, but there is something off about Hudson leaving without even telling Logan. Those two have barely been separated since we got here."

"Logan wrote a letter home today, so maybe he'll hear back soon," Kit says. "Maggie, your parents didn't write back yet, did they?"

Evelyn scoffs. "Our letters are probably just stuck in the bottom of some mail truck somewhere. I bet we'll make it home before they do."

I gasp.

"What is it?" Evelyn asks.

With my towel and bag in hand, I make a split decision and shake my head. "Nothing," I lie. "Just thought I saw a spider."

"Well, did you?" she asks.

"Spiders are our friends," Kit reminds us. "They're more afraid of us than you are of them."

I shake my head. "Just a piece of lint."

I have an idea, but it's risky. I'll probably get caught and I'll probably get in trouble. There's no point in dragging my friends down with me.

If I'm going to find out what happened to Hudson, I need to do it alone.

CHAPTER NINETEEN

I don't know how long it takes for Evelyn and Kit to fall asleep, but it feels like hours.

Normally we all lie in bed and talk for a long, long time until one by one we each doze off, but tonight I pretend to fall asleep immediately and even throw in a few snores for good measure.

Once I'm sure they're both fast asleep, I dig through my suitcase for the darkest clothes I have and come up with black bike shorts and a black sleep T-shirt with a dancing slice of pizza on it. After turning the shirt inside out and adding a black baseball hat, I'm as close to camouflaged as I'm ever going to be.

The moment I walk outside, I step off the path and into the trees. I hold my breath for a moment as Helen practically floats down the path, mumbling to herself.

Earlier, when Evelyn asked about my parents' letters, I realized how strange it was that they hadn't written back.

I could see them forgetting once or a case of lost mail even, but twice seems weird.

Heck, my mom even cried at the airport when she dropped me off. I'm pretty sure she wouldn't miss a chance to write me a sappy letter and send me an extra pair of clean underwear.

Once Helen is out of sight, I do my best to walk along the tree line, but it only goes so far, and eventually I have to run up the hill without cover.

Just as I make it to the crest of the hill, I drop to my belly. The lights are off at the Blood Bank and the cafeteria. The only light comes from Sylvia's Lotus tent, glowing in the darkness.

If I could just break into the mailbox, I could see if all of our letters are just stockpiling in there, which is what I suspect. Kids writing home to tell their parents how miserable they are is just plain old bad business for Sylvia. If kids complain to their parents about wanting to go home, then parents are going to show up and start asking for refunds.

Bracing myself, I push up from the ground, but then drop back down immediately because just a few feet ahead of me, Captain B comes walking up the path and toward the mailbox with a bag in her hand.

I almost just stand up and give myself away. She'd probably be upset with me for breaking curfew, but not that much.

Then I watch as she unlocks the box and dumps the letters in her bag.

"What in the world . . . ," I whisper.

The fact that she's the one handling all of our letters in and out of this place makes me feel at least a little bit better.

With the bag slung over her shoulder, she turns the corner behind the cafeteria, and I check to make sure the path is clear before following her.

I tiptoe behind her just in time to see Captain B—the only adult I've trusted here since day one—flip open the lid of the dumpster and toss the bag full of letters home into the trash.

I swallow a gasp, trying to piece together what I just saw. Surely that had to be a mistake? Captain B wouldn't just throw all of our letters away like that.

She continues on and I race behind her to check in the dumpster to see if maybe I got confused, but no . . . sitting right there alongside bags of half-eaten dinners and other scraps is a trash bag full of handwritten letters.

I nearly hoist myself in to fish out the letters myself and save them from their landfill death—she could have at least recycled!—but Captain B continues walking toward Sylvia's sound bath tent, and I have to know what's in there.

William stands outside the tent like a guard, looking stern in a way that sends a shiver down my spine.

Okay, that's weird.

I should turn back. Whatever is in there, I'm not supposed to see. If I just go back now, I won't get in trouble. I'll just finish out the time I have left here and I'll never have to know what's inside this bizarre tent.

The memory of Logan, totally distraught in my cabin, flashes through my brain.

I can't turn back now. I have to find Hudson.

"What's the password?" William asks Captain B.

"Your face looks like a butt," she says.

My jaw drops and I have to stop myself from snickering. That alone was worth sneaking out for! I never hear adults talk to each other like that. Even when they're secretly fighting, they always do it silently like they have to be some unified force against every kid in the room.

He rolls his eyes, reminding me of the sarcastic, not-so-kid-friendly camp counselor I recognize. "That's not the password."

"Four people are allowed in this tent and I'm one of them," Captain B tells him. "It doesn't matter what the password is and I'm pretty sure you just make it up so you can feel important for five minutes of your pathetic day."

Whoa, whoa, whoa. Maybe Captain B isn't as nice as I thought she was.

Eventually William steps aside, flopping his whole body around like she's asking him to do the dishes or something, and lets her in.

I have got to see what's happening in that tent, but I'm going to need a distraction.

After doubling back to the dumpster, I hold my nose as I dive inside. There has to be something in here that will help. I untie one bag and it doesn't take me long to find a giant half-eaten bowl of meatballs. *Yuck.*

With the bowl balanced in one hand, I swing my leg over the side, lose my footing, and come crashing down with an armful of meatballs.

The moment I realize how much noise I've made, I freeze. Unfortunately, I also get a whiff of myself and *ewwww* . . . Is that spaghetti sauce and zoodles in my hair?

"Who is that?" William yells out into the night.

With my breath held, I wait to see if I'm about to be found out, but after a moment, I peer around the corner to find he hasn't left his post.

Running as lightly as I can, I dart behind the back side of the tent and around Sylvia's trailer. For the first time I notice that the windows are completely blacked out with metal shades. This thing is built like a tank.

Once I've made it to the far end of her trailer, I wind my arm up just like I see the girls' softball team do at school, and then I toss a meatball as hard as I can, aiming for William— and BOOM! I hit him right in the head!

Maybe I should do a little less watching softball and a little more playing, but for right now, I have to do a whole lot of running. I sprint through the tree line, leaving a trail of meatballs behind me until I'm out of supplies, and then I cut across the trees to the back of the tent.

"Meatballs??" William screams in utter confusion. "Meatballs! Really?"

I crawl down on my belly and catch my breath for a

second before lifting up the very edge of the tent so that I can just barely see inside and still remain mostly hidden.

Directly in front of me is a set of feet adorned in red toenail polish and wearing white heeled sandals, which definitely belong to Sylvia. Near the entrance is Sloane. Steve the cameraman is nowhere to be seen.

Captain B sits in a chair at the edge of the tent with a very annoyed look on her face, but that's not the weirdest part.

Five people stand in a semicircle in front of Sylvia, floating a few inches above the ground.

It's like the air has been sucked out of my lungs. This can't be real. I have to be dreaming. I still don't know what a sound bath is, but I don't think this is it.

I must blink for two minutes straight. Maybe Sylvia's on some state-of-the-art hoverboard, or maybe the Scarlet Diet works so well that it turns you into an extraterrestrial being.

I force myself to focus for a minute and check out the other people in Sylvia's circle. Except they're not exactly *people*. They look more like fuzzy TV screens when the internet has a weak signal. In fact, they almost remind me of holograms from those old *Star Trek* episodes Dad is obsessed with.

A very tall woman in a long, red, off-the-shoulder dress lets out a deep groan. "Marcus, we can't do this every meeting. You would have better service if you sprang for 5G. It doesn't help that you live in the actual wilderness of Transylvania."

The man who I assume is Marcus, a gaunt, nearly skeletal figure who looks more like a giant old man/baby than an adult, wears a long black cloak. He cuts in and out and then just freezes mid-snarl. A bright purple vein cuts down the front of his forehead, and the sight of him alone is enough to make me shudder.

"He's frozen again, which is just as well. If I have to sit through another one of his rants about holding VampCon in Transylvania, I might just walk into direct sunlight," says a bored woman with an Australian accent and an intricate tattoo of a half-moon that frames her face.

VampCon? Like Comic-Con? But what does . . . surely, Sylvia isn't a . . .

My heart begins to race and I feel like I might puke . . . or maybe that's just because I smell like a dumpster.

The woman with the tattoo continues, "Can we just get on with this, Sylvia? It's nearly sunrise here and I have my beauty rest to think of."

Sylvia sighs and turns to Sloane. "Could you be a dear and send a batmail to Marcus with the minutes from our meeting?"

"If she's taking minutes, then what's the point of us even being here?" a man with a wiry mustache and a thick French accent asks.

"Because if we weren't here there would be no meeting, you numbskull," the woman in the red dress tells him. "Now, Sylvia, what updates do you have of your camp for plump children? Are they as juicy as you'd hoped? Has this mad endeavor proved to be worthwhile?"

Juicy? Maybe to mosquitoes? Sweat begins to gather at the back of my neck. There's no way this is a good thing.

Sylvia lets out an excited shriek. "Even more so! The high-iron diet and early curfew has created the perfect storm and business is *booming* at the Blood Bank."

"Hello?" Marcus calls. "Am I still connected?"

Ignore him the woman in red mouths to the rest of the group.

And, to be honest, I sort of agree. This Marcus guy seems like a real downer.

"Well," the Frenchman says, "when can we expect a sample? I do love the flavor of children. You mustn't tease me any longer. Can't we have just a taste?"

My eyes go so wide they feel like they might pop right out of my skull. The . . . the flavor of . . . ? Surely he doesn't mean . . . to eat? I think I might be sick.

"We're hard at work bottling our prototypes," Sylvia tells him. "We could be shipping globally in a matter of months."

I clap my hand over my mouth, because . . . Camp Sylvania isn't a weight-loss camp . . .

And these people aren't people. They're vampires.

This place is a living, breathing vending machine for vampires!

VAMPIRES!

Holy schnikes! My heart begins to thud so loudly that I

can practically hear it . . . and if I can hear my heartbeat, surely a tent full of vampires with superhuman abilities can too.

But what about William and Captain B? Sloane? Helen? Nurse Belinda? Does this mean they're all bloodsuckers?

"And what will you do when your sniveling blood supply goes back home to their pathetic parents?" asks the woman with the face tattoo.

Sylvia tsks. "Angelique, always the skeptic. Who said they're ever going home?"

I let out a soft, involuntary gasp as my jaw drops, and that's the exact moment when my gaze meets Captain B's.

She grimaces so fiercely I swear I hear a growl.

This is bad. Like end-of-the-world bad.

Or at least end of my world.

CHAPTER TWENTY

Run, run, run, run, run!

I veer off into the tree line as the tent flaps ripple open behind me.

Looking over my shoulder, I catch a glimpse of Captain B and William knocking foreheads.

"Watch it," Captain B tells him.

"Where are you going?" he asks her. "You look like a dead squirrel just crawled up your butt."

"And you look like a dead squirrel," she tells him.

He hisses in a way that makes me think he might not be entirely human.

I begin to run again, because I'm not about to end up between those two in the woods. Maybe Captain B didn't see me well enough to make out who was snooping. I was tucked away in the dark after all . . . but I still feel like my stomach is in my throat.

Maybe I can just fly under the radar until Parents' Day.

There's no way Sylvia can actually keep us here forever. Mom and Dad said so themselves at the airport that they'd see me at Parents' Day.

As I weave in and out of the trees, I glance over my shoulder to see someone—no, something—chasing me. It's like a shadowy fog that's slow moving and yet somehow only a few feet behind me. Even though I'm sweating and it's a muggy night, the air at my back begins to feel cold. Can vampires turn into fog?

I make a split-second decision to cut back onto the path. At least from there, I can scream for help and stand a chance at waking up other campers.

When I make it back to the path, I look behind me once more, and the figure is gone, but all that means is I can't see it.

As I speed walk to my cabin I decide that if a counselor stops me, I can say I had to go to the bathroom. But running right now would definitely look suspicious, and the last thing I need is a run-in with Helen. Thankfully my beloved Cabin Three is just a few steps away.

Breathing a sigh of relief, I open my door and immediately lock it behind me, though I'm pretty sure that's not going to do anything against a camp staffed by vampires.

I don't even bother changing into my pajamas. Instead I take a running leap into my bed, like I would do when I was a little kid in case there were any monsters lurking under my mattress, ready to yank me into the darkness.

Except this time, not even my bed feels safe. I tremble at every creaking tree branch and whistle of wind. Because I can't bring myself to look out into our room and risk my imagination filling in what might be hiding in a dark corner, I stare up at the ceiling of our cabin for the rest of the night, hoping that this has all been a bad dream.

"Hello in there," a voice calls from outside the door. Helen's voice. "Be a dear and invite me inside. I only want to talk."

I squeeze my eyes shut and think of home. I think of Nora. And school. And even the kids who have made fun of me or purposefully not invited me to their birthday parties. I think of bombing when I took the stage in *Annie*.

I think of anything and everything I can that reminds me of my life outside of this place as I hear footfalls circling our cabin. Helen whispers over and over again. "One, two, three . . . one, two, three . . ."

I don't doze off until the sky outside begins to glow with the promise of sunrise, but it's only for a few minutes. The memory of last night and the absolutely impossible things I saw and heard are enough to drag me out of bed.

Evelyn and Kit, who are already dressed, wait for me outside.

"Hey, we're going to meet you up there," Evelyn says. "Logan's walking by himself, and he looks like he needs company."

"Okay," I call to them. "I'll catch up in a minute."

I peer out the screen window on the door as they run to meet him. I promised Logan answers and somehow after last night, I still have no clue what happened to Hudson. But my head is definitely heavy with some very scary theories.

After I put on my uniform, I follow the path up to the cafeteria and rec area. It's impossible not to see this place in a whole new light. No one here can be trusted. Not even Captain B.

As I walk past the craft barn, I step over to the far side of the path, closest to the trees.

I'm gonna have to see Captain B sooner than later, but when I do, I'm hoping I won't be alone and—

Something reaches out from the trees and yanks me into the woods, and my head is immediately filled with all the awful things that could happen to me. All the things that probably already happened to Hudson.

"Shhhh," a voice whispers.

I open my mouth to scream, but a rag is shoved in my mouth and I fall asleep faster than I do at night in the back seat of a car.

My last thought is of my parents. I see their silhouettes in the front seat of our car, their hands linked together.

I think this camp might just kill me.

My eyes flutter as I slowly wake up. I try to talk, but the rag is still in my mouth so all that comes out is a garbled mess.

I wiggle around enough to know I'm in an office chair and my wrists are tied to the armrests.

Slowly, my vision comes into focus and I find that I'm in the craft barn. All around me are Captain B's various woodworking projects, set pieces, and half-sewn costumes.

I feel like I'm in a movie, and with my feet tied at the ankles, it's a little tricky, but I throw my body forward as hard as I can, so that maybe I'll roll close enough to one of the tables and grab one of her tools to free—

Captain B steps out of the shadows, into a patch of sunlight, and my whole body wrenches backward.

Her fists are clenched and she looks like she's ready to drink every last drop of blood in my body.

I scream as loudly as I can, but it's muffled and when I try to call her a *vampire*, it comes out like "Wam pie!"

"I can't untie you or pull that thing out of your mouth unless I know you're not going to scream," she says calmly.

I breathe in and out and in and out, trying to regain my cool—or at least look like I have. I refuse to die in a barn. Especially before I've starred in a show without choking, or ridden a Jet Ski.

She steps forward. "Now, are you going to scream?"

I shake my head, even though I'm totally going to scream.

"I know you're lying," she tells me, "so let's just get this out of the way: I'm not a vampire." She pulls the rag out of my mouth. "I just work for them. Sort of."

Okay, so maybe if she's not a vampire then at least she can't eat me, so maybe I won't scream. Yet. "So this means you can't drink my blood, right?"

Captain B laughs as she begins to untie my hands. "Blood isn't really my beverage of choice."

"Okay. Fine. Where is Hudson then?"

"Hudson?" She shrugs. "He went home early."

If she's not going to tell me the truth, then I'm getting out of here. I stand up and immediately fall face-first on the floor with a loud *thwack*.

"Feet," she says helpfully. "Still tied together."

I roll over with a grunt, and pull my legs in so I can untie myself.

She sits on the chair I was just on and fidgets with a pencil on her desk. "I'm surprised you don't have any other questions for me. It was chloroform, by the way. That's what made you pass out, though I'm still not sure how I feel about that on a moral level."

"Yeah, me neither," I spit back at her, even though it felt just like when they put me under to remove my tonsils last winter break. "And maybe if you didn't lie to me about Hudson, I would bother asking you more." I shake the rope off my ankles and stand. "I thought you were one of the good ones, Captain B. But adults are all the same. You're untrustworthy and hypocritical. You expect kids to be all the things you aren't." I turn and stomp toward the exit.

I'm going to remember this moment for as long as I live and when I'm the adult in the room, I'll do everything I can to give the kids I know what they deserve: honesty.

"Wait," Captain B calls after me.

I look back over my shoulder.

"Just wait," she says like she's given up. "I'll tell you what I know, but you have to believe me when I tell you that when it comes to Hudson—and every other camper who's gone home early, I know as much as you do." She pulls a block of wood over for me to sit on and pats the top. "You're gonna want to sit down for this."

With my guard as high up as it will go, I walk back over and sit down across from her. "Talk."

CHAPTER TWENTY-ONE

"Sylvia is my sister," she blurts.

My jaw drops. "You . . . her . . . you two are related?"

"Actually, she's my twin . . . fraternal twin to be clear."
She sounds like she's confessing a secret.

"Is that the kind of twins who don't look alike?" I ask.

She nods. "And my real name is Birdie."

I gasp so hard I almost choke. "*You're* Birdie?" I ask. "You
knew my mom! She said you all were close, but she never
said her roommates were *twins*."

She leans back in her chair, a stunned expression slapped
on her face. "You're Sofia's daughter? You—I heard she'd
gotten married and changed her last name . . . but it never
crossed my mind that you . . . you could be her daughter."

My cheeks warm. "The one and only daughter of THE
Sofia Hagen. In the flesh! She showed me so many pictures
of you three . . . you all looked so happy."

Birdie inhales deeply. "Sylvia wasn't always like this . . .

but being her twin hasn't been fun for a long, long time. Even before she turned into a vampire," she tells me. "She's always had a way of finding the things I love in life and stealing them from me. Like this camp."

"This place?" I ask.

"I'd been saving to buy the camp for years. I was going to turn this place into a safe zone for all kinds of kids, but especially fat kids. I had some bad times at Camp New Beginnings, but it was also the first place where I felt totally normal. I didn't stand out. At fat camp, fat was the normal. And that's why I stuck around for so long. I wanted to take my good memories here and make a place where you could look any way or be anyone and still fit in."

I find myself nodding along with her, because even though the last two weeks have felt like hell, I've experienced exactly what she's talking about. Especially the other day at the lake. "Does Sylvia know you use the *F* word so much?"

Captain B rolls her eyes. "The only thing wrong with the word *fat* is that Sylvia thinks it's something to be scared of. There's nothing wrong with our bodies, Maggie. Don't you forget that. There's nothing wrong with you." She reaches toward me, like she might just touch my face. "I can't believe it took me so long to see it, but you look just like her."

I can't help but want to trust her, especially now that I know who she really is. Even though I'm still scared that Captain B might just be lying about this whole thing and actually be a vampire herself, her words make me feel like I'm glowing inside. When I was little, I remember people called my pudgy legs and chubby arms cute, but in the last few years the *awwws* have turned into looks of concern. Something about the way Captain B talks makes me feel sure of myself . . . maybe for the first time ever.

She continues, "Anyway, Sylvia heard the place was for sale and swooped in with an offer the owners couldn't refuse."

"That stinks," I say. "But how does the whole vampire thing make sense?"

"Buckle up. Things are about to get weird." She leans back in her chair. "Sylvia isn't kidding when she says she used to be fat. You saw the pictures. Ever since she lost that weight, she's lived in fear of being that person again. It terrifies her. She's always chasing the latest weight-loss method or drug or diet. Anything she can do to ensure she never goes back to looking like . . . well, me. She started getting into some weird things and became obsessed with immortality, and she even went through a phase where she thought she could freeze her body . . . like some kind of sci-fi book. And then she met Helen."

"Helen?" I ask. "The night counselor?"

She clasps her hands together. "Helen works for the Council—all those vampires you saw. She turned Sylvia. For a price. I guess Sylvia was onto something, because it turns out immortality isn't as impossible as we're taught to believe.

If she could just have the perfect body, she'd found a way to keep it perfect forever."

I hold up a hand. "Okay. So vampires are for sure real then?" I think I'd been holding out some kind of hope that this was all some mistake or even an elaborate inside joke.

"Yeah, they've been walking this planet just as long we have. Probably longer." She shivers and makes a gagging noise. "Marcus is one of the Ancients. You saw him on her holo-call."

"The one with the bad connection?" I ask with a laugh.

She half smiles, half grimaces. "That's the one. When they set up an email address for him a few months ago, he opened some junk mail asking for his banking information so that they could transfer him money he'd supposedly won on a cruise ship and he actually sent it! Vampires don't even go on cruises. Anyway, the Council used to meet every few months in person, but Sylvia is determined to bring modern technology to vampirism."

"So she's on the Council?" I ask.

"Oh, no, no. She's . . . Let's just say my sister likes to walk into a room and immediately become a big fish."

I know exactly what she means. It's like the kind of kid who can show up to a new school and be popular immediately. Or even like the professor in *The Music Man*. "Does that mean she's just a baby vampire?"

"Technically, but don't let yourself underestimate her. I don't think she has any plans of stopping with this camp. In fact, if I were on the Council, I'd watch my back. One thing I'll say about my twin is that she's determined. You've seen the way she can convince people. She tracked down the Council within weeks of turning and made her case. She wants to make this camp basically the Coca-Cola of vampire beverage manufacturing. It's the perfect cover. Kids get dropped off here for weeks at a time and their parents basically forget they exist."

Something in me twinges at the thought of my parents forgetting who I am. "It sure feels like that," I tell her. "Throwing away our letters doesn't help."

She sighs with remorse. "So you saw that, huh?"

"Yup."

"I don't throw them away because I want to. I do it because the only way for me to defeat her is to join her. When she showed up here it didn't take long for me to figure out what was going on, so I had to make her think I was all-in and that I wanted to be a vampire too."

"But you don't, do you?" I ask, still unable to fully trust her even though I really, really want to.

Captain B lets out a big belly laugh. "I couldn't even if I wanted to. Sylvia has said she won't turn me until I reach my goal weight."

I can't help but laugh at that. Of course Sylvia would say that. "No offense, but your sister is the worst."

Captain B rolls her eyes. "That's not even half of it."

"What about Sloane and William? Steve the cameraman?"

She leans forward. "And her camera guy is just some random dude she hired to capture some content. He has no idea how much danger he'd be in if he captured the *wrong* kind of content. And Sloane and William are what we call familiars."

I don't even know what that means, but my brain is racing. With every piece of information Captain B shares, I can't help but feel like I have more questions than I do answers. "So why the camp?" I ask. "Why the Blood Bank?"

"Her blood debt," she says. "When a new vampire is turned they have to bring a sacrifice to pay their debt to the Council, but like I said, Sylvia has bigger—"

Light leaks in behind us as the barn door slides open. "There you are," Sloane says with her hands on her hips. "You had us worried, Maggie."

My heart stutters. Does Sloane have vampire powers even though she's a . . . what was it? A familiar! Do vampires know when you're lying? Do vampires even like musical theater? "Uhhhh . . . I, uh . . ."

"Maggie tripped outside the barn," Captain B says. "I was just giving her time to rest before—"

"You should have taken her to the nurse," Sloane says sternly.

Even vampire henchwomen are like every other adult I know. Always talking about you like you're not there.

"You're right," Captain B tells her. "I'll keep that in mind next time."

I stand up. "I better get back." I smile at Sloane a little too widely as sweat beads down my spine. *Please don't eat me.*

She smiles back, but it's more of a snarl and I squeeze past her, taking off down the trail as fast as I can.

I rejoin the rest of my campers, who are absolutely melting under the much-too-hot morning sun, and for the first time in my life, I'm thankful to be racing up and down this awful hill in a crowd of other kids as William blows on his whistle.

Surely there's safety in numbers. . . .

CHAPTER TWENTY-TWO

After our morning workouts, I return to my cabin. I have to find Captain B—or Birdie—again and I need to do some investigating of my own, and to do that, I want to put together a few very necessary supplies. Flashlight, notebook, and the walking stick I made just a few days ago.

I don't know what I'm going to do with this giant stick and I can't think too much about that, but I do know I need some kind of protection. And I think Birdie thought that too.

It's like the first time I went to the optometrist and they made me look through all these different lenses until the letters on the eye test came into focus. Maybe Birdie's insistence on the earlier curfew and all her carvings and walking sticks had nothing to do with bear safety or arts and crafts.

And I think I've only just scratched the surface. There's so much going on here at this camp that I just wrote off as odd because never in my life could I imagine vampires actually being real.

"Care to explain why you're sneaking off without us all of a sudden?" Evelyn asks, with her arms crossed, as she and Kit walk through the door.

"Y'all are missing lunch," I say, genuinely confused.

Kit crosses her arms over her chest too. "And you're not? We know you snuck out last night."

"And you showed up late this morning," Evelyn adds. "William said that tomorrow we have to run three extra laps because our whole cabin wasn't there."

"I'm really sorry," I say. "I'll do something to make it up. I swear."

Evelyn eyes the supplies I've laid out on my mattress. "How about you start with telling us what you're up to?"

I sit down on the edge of my bed. "We only have a week left here, okay? I don't want to get either of you in any trouble . . . or in any danger."

"Danger?" Evelyn asks. "I daresay the most dangerous thing here is the insect population."

I shake my head. "Just please trust me." My whole body tenses up at the thought of anything happening to either of them. Maybe the best thing for us all to do is just to survive this and go home like nothing happened.

"Oh, Maggie," Kit says. "I don't really have a lot of friends back home, and already the both of you feel more like besties than anyone else I know. And besties don't keep secrets. We don't want you to hide anything from us, right, Evelyn? We can handle it. Whatever it is."

Evelyn nods as she comes to sit down next to me. "Kit's right. And yeah, the only good thing about this place is getting two new besties."

Kit grins at that, her cheeks turning a soft shade of pink.

"Listen," Evelyn says. "If you're in trouble, we're in trouble. And if you're in danger, we're right there with you. Whatever is going on, you don't have to go through it alone."

"Kit," I say, motioning to the empty spot on my other side. "You might want to sit down."

She does and even takes her conversation heart candy pillow that says LOL in her lap in anticipation of what I'm going to say. I wish I'd been cuddling my pillow when I found out what I'm about to tell them.

I take a deep breath. "Okay, what do y'all know about vampires?"

It takes a while to explain everything, especially when I don't even have the full story.

"Okay, but did you happen to find out what else is real?" Kit asks. "Like, are we talking werewolves? Ghosts? Aliens? Zombies?"

"Really?" I ask. "That's your first question."

"It's just the first one that came out of my mouth," she explains.

"I didn't exactly get that far," I tell her.

She thinks for a moment before thoughtfully adding, "I wonder if vampires are related to mosquitoes."

Evelyn hasn't said a word since I dropped the vamp bomb. "Are you okay?" I ask her. "I know this is a lot to process, but I think this is totally linked to Hudson going missing . . . and other campers too maybe. And what about Charlotte and Tori?"

Her eyes are glistening. "Yeah. Yeah. I just . . . I wish I'd trusted my gut. I knew something was wrong. It's like when my parents got divorced. I saw all the signs, but I didn't want it to be true, so I ignored it. I knew something was up the moment they said we were doing a blood donation drive. It just didn't add up. And then . . ."

Kit looks from Evelyn to me. Neither of us has ever seen Evelyn like this. She's always so sure of herself.

"Did you see something?" I ask. "You can tell us."

"I thought it was my imagination," she says, her head shaking. "But one night I went to the bathroom by myself . . . and I thought I saw Helen chasing after a deer. . . . She caught it and it was gruesome. . . . I ran back to our bunk and the next morning I'd convinced myself it was a bad dream."

"Oh my gosh, that's so scary." I put an arm around her shoulder. "Wait. Was that the other day when you said you didn't sleep well?"

She nods as tears begin to spill.

"Does this mean all of our counselors are vampires?" Kit asks.

I think on that for a minute. Captain B isn't one. I don't think William or Sloane are either. . . . "I can't be sure, but it sounds like it's not all of them. I think it's safe to say Helen is. In fact, I know she is. She's the one who turned Sylvia into a vampire."

"She might be scarier than Sylvia herself," Evelyn says softly.

"I've never seen her during the day," I add. "But we do see Sylvia during the day, so I'm not sure what to make of that."

Evelyn finally lifts her gaze from the floor. "Never in direct sunlight, though." She picks up my walking stick and examines it. "Do you think wooden stakes work on them? Like in the movies."

I shrug. "Maybe, but I think we need to talk to Captain B."

"I wish we could get on the internet," Kit says. "It's like I think I know all this stuff about vampires, but all I can think of is *Twilight*."

Evelyn laughs at that. "Yeah, these vampires definitely don't sparkle."

I'm really kicking myself for not reading Dad's Vampire Underground series now, and I make a mental note to bump those books up my summer reading list when I get home—if I get home. "We might not have the internet," I say, "but between the three of us, I bet we've seen enough movies and

read enough books to at least make a list of what we know."
I reach for my notebook. Too bad I can't go back in time and
actually listen when Dad spent so many dinners trying to
work out the plot of his next book with Mom. "So what do
we know?"

"Bats!" Kit says. "They turn into bats."

I write it down, even though I can't imagine Sylvia or
Helen or anyone for that matter turning into a tiny flying
creature. But I guess until yesterday I couldn't imagine being
trapped at a camp run by vampires.

"Mirrors!" Evelyn says. "They can't see themselves."

I gasp. "Oh, oh! They have to be asked inside of a house."

"This isn't a house, though." Kit's brows furrow like she's
trying to solve a puzzle.

"It is to us," Evelyn says with authority. "Suddenly some
of these camps rules are starting to make more sense."

"You're right," I agree. "Helen can't come in here unless
we ask her in. Just the other night she stood outside our
door, asking to be let in."

Both of their jaws drop in unison, and after a moment,
Kit's whole body convulses in a shiver.

"That's the kind of thing nightmares are made of," Evelyn
whispers.

"I pretended to be asleep. It was the night I saw Sylvia
meeting with the Council," I explain.

"Do they know that you know?" asks Kit.

I nervously doodle on the edge of my notebook paper. "I'm not sure. At first, I thought for sure they knew, but I guess I probably wouldn't be here anymore if that was really true."

The three of us sit there in silence as the reality of the situation washes over us.

"I've got one more bomb to drop," I tell them. "Captain B's real name is Birdie and she's Sylvia's sister."

Their jaws go slack. I've completely stunned them.

"Sisters as in two human beings—or one vampire and one human being—who are related? By blood?" Evelyn asks.

"Yup," I tell them before explaining the whole story about this camp and even how my mom went here.

"This sort of feels like walking in on your parents fighting," Evelyn says. "Except one of them is a vampire."

Evelyn stares out our screen window, forlorn. "How do you even win against a vampire? Especially one like Sylvia."

We both stare into space for a moment, because this problem feels so much bigger than any of us and it's hard not to feel like we're already doomed.

"The list," Kit finally says. "Let's focus on what we can do, and what we can do is start with this list."

"You're right." Evelyn takes a deep breath. "So what do we know?"

After a while of putting our heads together, our list looks like this:

- Bats!
- No reflection in mirrors
- Can be killed with wooden stakes
- Allergic to holy water (sidenote: How do you make water holy? Can you make it or is it already holy?)
- Sleep (rest?) during the day in coffins
- Live on a diet of blood
- garlic = bad
- Pointy teeth?
- Can only come into a home if invited in
- Can't cross water? (Kit thinks so, but not sure. Maggie thinks it's in her dad's book.)
- Cannot cross a line of salt (or maybe it's sugar?)

"What are we supposed to do?" Evelyn asks as we study our list. "I mean, you can't just like . . . call the Secret Service or something."

"Are they hurting anyone?" Kit asks. "Maybe the Blood Bank is so they don't have to hurt people anymore? Not all vampires are bad, right?"

"People are *missing*," I say. "Hudson is missing."

They both look at me like I'm supposed to have a plan, but I definitely do not have a plan. There are zero plans in my brain!

"This is what I know," I finally say. "If we don't want to also go missing, we need to keep things business as usual. So during the day, we do all of our normal stuff and be model campers . . . but we also always stick together because it's harder to make three kids disappear than it is one."

Kit takes my hand and then Evelyn's. "What's the worst that could happen in a week?"

Evelyn sighs. "It might be best if we didn't try to answer that question."

CHAPTER TWENTY-THREE

Just like we said we would, we keep to our routines, which includes donating blood—and donating blood takes on a whole new meaning for us.

I watch as Nurse Belinda presses the needle into my arm, and all I can think about is how some vampire is probably going to use my blood to make their morning smoothie.

She catches me staring. "Everything all right, dear?"

I can feel Evelyn's and Kit's eyes on me. "Oh yes. Just thinking about how many people all of us campers must be helping with our donations. Wouldn't it be amazing if there was some sort of way to see how much good we're doing?"

Nurse Belinda smiles. "The most selfless deeds are those done quietly."

"I couldn't agree more," Evelyn chimes in. "But I was just thinking of the summer report I'll write when I go back to school in the fall, and I'm sure my teacher would be so interested to hear about this program."

Nurse Belinda's smile slowly slips into something almost sinister and she says, "I'm sure you can adequately explain our Blood Bank without jeopardizing the privacy of our recipients."

Evelyn nods with a forced smile, and once Nurse Belinda goes back to her desk, we all share a panicked look.

I'd hoped the supersweet nurse wasn't in on sucking us human campers dry, but I don't see how she couldn't be.

Nurse Belinda's phone begins to ring. She answers it and quickly hangs up. "Girls, I'll be right back."

Leaning forward in my seat, I watch the door, waiting for it to close completely before I hop up and yank the needle out of my arm.

Kit's eyes widen. "Maggie! What are you doing?"

I run quickly down to the end of the trailer where a huge refrigerator sits and, unfortunately, I don't think it's full of Popsicles. "All of our blood has to be going somewhere. Maybe I can find a clue. Keep an eye out," I tell them.

When I open the heavy double doors of the refrigerator, I find bottles and bottles full of blood in perfectly straight lines. The sight of it shouldn't surprise me, but it certainly freaks me out.

I pull one bottle off the shelf to find it wrapped in a colorful label that reads *ETERNAL ELIXIR* and then in smaller letters: *HARVESTED FROM THE FINEST, PLUMPEST CHILDREN. MADE IN THE USA.*

Each lid is dated and labeled with a specific blood type.

Maybe vampires can taste the difference?

I don't know what Sylvia has planned, but it looks like her ambitions haven't changed much since becoming immortal.

"Maggie!" Evelyn calls. "I think I hear something."

I put the bottle back and race over to my seat.

Kit makes a jittery circle with her hand, like it's time to wrap it up. "What are you going to do about—"

The door to the trailer swings open, and I hold my arm to my chest. "Oh, Nurse Belinda," I say, "thank goodness you're back! My tablet fell over and I must have reached too far and . . ." I motion to the mess I've made.

"Oh, dear," she says with a tsk. "I always tell them I can't leave my station, but do they listen? No."

She putters over to me and reinserts the needle with ease.

"Thank you so much," I tell her.

With glassy eyes and a too perfect smile, she says, "Oh, it's my pleasure. Truly." She walks back over to her desk and takes her thermos to the back of the trailer, where I hear the refrigerator doors open followed by a *glug-glug-glug* sound.

Nurse Belinda returns, sipping from the metal straw of her thermos. "You girls should be nearly done. Don't forget to fill up on snacks before you leave. Yummy!"

The next afternoon, we venture out to the craft barn and do our best to carry ourselves like it's any normal day.

But nothing about today is normal.

We need to find Birdie. We need to find answers.

"Maybe we can crochet today," Kit says a little too loudly. "Or paint serene watercolor scenes."

"I think you're trying to act a little too normal," I whisper to her. "Like, now it's just weird."

"Uh, Maggie?" Evelyn says as she approaches the craft barn. "Kit?"

We catch up to her and find the barn door is chained shut. A white piece of paper is taped just above the padlock and in bright red ink, the sign reads CRAFT BARN CLOSED FOR CRAFTING UNTIL FURTHER NOTICE.

We circle around the building, peeking into the window near Birdie's desk. Everything is just the way it was when I was last here. Even the block of wood she pulled up for me to sit on is still right where I left it.

"Maybe crafts just moved to another building?" Kit says, and even her normally hopeful mood is dwindling.

"I don't know. This feels off," I say.

Evelyn peers through the crack in the door. "I still can't believe she and Sylvia are sisters."

"Looks like we've got some snooping snoopers," someone says.

The three of us spin around to find Sloane standing on the path with William alongside her.

"Surely you saw the sign on the barn door," Sloane says. "So I guess in a way, you three are trespassing. Don't you think, William?"

"Definitely trespassing," William confirms.

"Um, I don't think that's what trespassing means . . . especially since we're campers and this is camp property," Kit tells them with her hands on her hips.

"Oh, she's a lawyer," William says. "Someone call the judge. We've got a smarty-pants lawyer on our hands."

Sloane fakes a gasp. "Oh no, a lawyer. So scary. What if she tries to sue us?"

I roll my eyes. "We get it, okay? Now where's Captain B?" I ask, looking right at her. I know I just said we need to play it as cool as possible, but if something happened to Captain B, I'm pretty sure these two had something to do with it.

"She quit," Sloane says simply. "Didn't even put in a two weeks' notice. Very irresponsible if you ask me. Now, better go find something to keep you busy until rehearsal."

William makes a shooing motion with his hand.

The two of them walk off, and without looking back, William calls, "Better yet, you could practice. You need all the practice you can get, Maggie."

WEEK THREE OF CAMP

CHAPTER TWENTY-FOUR

"Don't worry," Evelyn tells me. "Shows always come together at the last moment."

The whole vampire thing has kept my mind off my nerves, but it's also been a huge distraction, and it's starting to show. Sunday's rehearsal was disastrous and today's was somehow worse. I was all jumpy and in my head for obvious reasons, and Logan was upset because he was worried about his brother. I missed most of my cues and when I *was* onstage, I could hardly remember my lines.

Despite the yelling and constant taunting, I think Sloane and William might have secretly enjoyed how awful things were going. Being in a musical directed by that duo is like living with a nonstop loop of snarky reality TV judges. Zero stars out of ten. I do not recommend.

"Were you able to dig up anything on what happened to Birdie?" I ask as we wait outside the shower stalls for Kit to finish up.

Evelyn tucks a few loose strands into her bonnet. "I tried. So did Kit. But William kept pointing at his eyes like this." She holds two fingers right below her eyes. "And then pointing at me and telling me 'A stage manager never abandons their post.'"

Kit turns the corner as she ties the drawstring on her pajama shorts. "What are we even looking for?" Her voice drops to a whisper. "Surely there's not just some vampire handbook lying around waiting to be discovered."

I wait until we're a few feet down the path toward our cabin to answer her. "We're looking for anything! Captain B said she was fighting against them . . . so there has to be something. Some sort of hint."

Kit nods. "She was always so busy in that barn. And I think we might have been the only ones who ever went in there for crafts."

"Maybe she was planning something big," Evelyn says. "Maybe she still is and she left on her own to go get help or something."

I glance up as we step off the path for our cabin, and at the tree line where the camp property ends, a brief but bright flash of movement vanishes into the darkness. "Did either of you see that?" I ask.

They both look up.

Kit's head tilts to the side. "See wha—"

Evelyn gasps and steps back. "Is that . . ."

At the edge of the tree line, a figure steps forward. A

boy . . . sort of. He looks more like a watery shadow than any human thing I've ever seen. Almost like he's made of . . . fog! Just like whatever was chasing me the other night! His blond curly hair is soaked in moonlight and his neon-yellow swim trunks and tie-dyed tank top are bright but muted.

"Howie Wowie," I whisper.

The three of us stand there in a frozen stupor. First, vampires are real. Now ghosts.

"Uh-uh," Evelyn says. "Nope. Let's go to our cabin and pretend we never even saw this."

"He looks friendly," Kit says, like this is no big deal.

"He pulls kids under the water. Even Captain B said so! And what if this isn't even Howie?" Evelyn shakes her head and begins to backpedal.

I guess there's a chance this isn't Howie, but—

Slowly, he raises his hand and we all huddle together for safety like he might just throw some kind of ghostly goo our way, but that's not what he does. Not at all.

"I think he's waving," Kit whispers.

I step just a few feet away from them for a closer look, but Howie's hand isn't moving side to side. It's moving back and forth. "He's calling us," I say. "He wants to show us something."

Evelyn's shoulders tense. "I'm pretty sure this is how people die in horror films."

"He's one of us," Kit says. "Or at least he used to be."

"She's right," I tell Evelyn. "Besides, Birdie said he warns campers not to go swimming at night. That sounds like a pretty nice ghost if you ask me."

"I'm pretty sure she said he asks campers to go swimming *with* him," I say.

Kit nudges me in the ribs with her elbow.

"And anyway," I add, "it's three against one."

Kit loops her arm through Evelyn's. "We stick together, remember?"

With a sigh, Evelyn links arms with me. "Together."

And with that, the three of us step across the path and into the dark, dark night.

Every time we step closer to Howie, he disappears a little farther into the woods.

"What if we can't find our way back?" Evelyn asks.

"I have the stars," Kit tells her, "and you have an expert Girl Scout at your disposal."

I run a few feet ahead of them, nervous that we might lose him.

Evelyn glances behind us. "I can't even see the lake anymore."

"That doesn't mean it's not there. It's just really overgrown here," I say. Howie cuts to the left, and I trip over the roots of a huge pine tree as I chase him. My knees hit the dirt with a sting and I catch myself with the palms of my hands.

"Are you okay?" Kit and Evelyn both ask as they come up behind me.

"Where'd he go?" I ask as I push off from the forest floor, not bothering to check for any scrapes, and peer around the tree.

Then I see it. The exact place Howie must be leading us to.

"Maybe he's just playing games with us . . . ," Evelyn says as she steps forward, her voice drifting off. "Is that another . . . cabin?"

Kit looks over our shoulders. "It has a thirteen on the door."

And sure enough, the dilapidated cabin that is barely standing has a 1 and a lopsided 3 hanging on the front door. Trees and brush have grown over the fading building to the point that this little structure looks like it was more likely made by the forest than it was by people.

"This is Cabin Thirteen," I whisper. "This was Howie's cabin."

"I thought Captain B said this cabin was long gone," Kit says.

Evelyn shivers. "This place looks pretty destroyed if you ask me."

I step forward. "Come on. We didn't come all the way here not to go in."

"This truly feels like a trap," Evelyn says through a moan.

I look around for a moment just to make sure that Howie is really and truly gone before I creep toward the door. Kit files in behind me and Evelyn holds on tight to her waist, hiding behind the both of us.

I pull on the door handle, and the rickety hinges let out a loud creak as we walk inside. "Shoot," I whisper. "I forgot my flashlight."

"Me too," they both say in unison.

The moon shines in through holes in the ceiling, casting small slivers of light across the floor, and I can make out some rusted bunk beds along the back wall and a floor littered with leaves and random trash.

"Hello?" I ask in a small voice.

The cabin door slams shut behind us with a loud rattle.

We let out a chorus of shrieks and I can't help but remember the time we found Helen lurking in the old computer lab. Maybe Howie has led us to her lair and we're nothing more than her midnight snack.

Wind rustles in the trees above, spinning the leaves and trash into a little cyclone all around us, and I swear I hear a voice in the wind say, "Shhhhhhh."

The wind settles and everything drops to the floor in a split second.

I can feel Kit and Evelyn watching me, waiting for me to do something—anything. I am the one who dragged us out here after all. "Howie?" I finally whisper. "Are you here with us?"

The leaves on the floor suddenly scatter to the edges of the room, and then slowly a few at a time drift toward the center, swirling in patterns and shapes before finally spelling HELLO.

"He can hear us?" Evelyn asks.

The leaves reform into a **YES**.

A thrill of excitement runs through me. My dad would absolutely die if he saw this! One year, Mom and I made him a birthday cake that looked like a Ouija board.

We look at each other, and I see just what I'm feeling reflected back to me in Evelyn's and Kit's eyes. Terror mixed with exhilaration.

Evelyn clears her throat, and balls her hands into fists at her sides. "Why did you bring us out here?"

"Good job," I whisper.

I hold my breath as the leaves begin to glide across the floor again. The way they move is so fluid that even though they're just dry and crunchy leaves, it almost looks like water.

The leaves settle, spelling out the next word. **WARN**.

"Warn," Kit whispers. "Warn against what?"

I swear my heart stops beating as we wait for his answer. No one can move through this camp like Howie can. He must see and hear . . . everything. (Oh gosh. Including last Saturday when I hid behind the tree next to the barn to let out the fart I'd been holding in during rehearsal. . . .) I can't begin to imagine what he might know, and what it might feel like to have no way of telling anyone.

PARENTS' DAY

"Parents' Day?" I ask. "What's going to happen then?"

FORGET

"Forget who?" Evelyn asks, her voice weary.

181

YOU

Kit snickers. "I think Howie just delivered a sick burn. Forget you? What did Evelyn ever do to him?"

I want to laugh, because the idea of a tie-dyed-wearing ghost insulting Evelyn is hilarious . . . but bile begins to rise in my stomach at the thought of what Howie might actually mean. "He's not talking to Evelyn," I say. "He's talking about Evelyn. He's talking about all of us." I try to gulp down my dread, but my throat is too dry.

"Forget us," Evelyn says softly. "Our parents are going to forget us?"

Kit's chin begins to tremble as what Howie is saying dawns on her.

"Howie, is that right? Is Sylvia going to make our parents forget us on Parents' Day?"

For a moment, the leaves don't move.

And then more frantically, and less graceful than they were before, they spell out **YES**.

"This can't be real," Kit says. "How can she—"

But before Kit can finish her sentence, a chaotic gust of wind blows the door open and the leaves quickly scatter into a new word.

RUN

CHAPTER TWENTY-FIVE

We don't think twice as we sprint out of the cabin. Without Howie here to lead us through the woods, the three of us do our best to retrace our steps, but we're completely lost. We try to remain calm, go fast, and find our way, but those three things are not easy to do all at once.

"The trees are too heavy for me to even see the sky," Kit says through short breaths as she and Evelyn follow close behind.

"It's okay," I tell her. "I think I know where we're going." Even though that is definitely *not* true. The once muggy air feels almost chilly, just like it had that night in the woods when I discovered the reality of this place, and our slippers and pajama pants are covered in mud and dirt.

"Do you two smell that?" Evelyn asks.

I sniff under my armpit as we continue to run. "I definitely should have reapplied deodorant today."

She wrinkles her nose. "No, not that."

I stop for a moment to try to get a whiff. The trees rustle above us and a strong, pungent smell drifts across my nostrils.

We slow down a bit and Kit follows the smell for a few feet and then crouches down to pluck something from the ground, holding it close to her nose. "Wild garlic," she says. "We're in a whole patch of it."

All around us are white twinkling flowers that seem to reflect the moonlight seeping through the trees. The flowers smell so strongly that the scent just might be burned to the inside of my nostrils forever.

Kit yanks another handful to examine it more closely.

A few feet behind us, leaves crunch, and I swear I see a dark shadow dart between the trees alongside us.

"I don't think we really have time to admire organic clover or whatever," I say.

Kit stuffs the plant in her pocket, and the three us follow the thinning line of trees until we break free of the woods and find ourselves back on the camp path.

"We have to sabotage Parents' Day," I announce, once it feels like we're in the clear.

"I can't imagine living in a world where my parents had just *forgotten* me." Kit sighs. "I feel so awful for Howie. Do you think he's just trapped here? Forever?"

My chest tightens at the thought. I didn't realize there could be something even more horrifying than bloodsucking vampires, but the idea that we could just be forgotten and left here to be breathing blood bags for Sylvia and her Council is a thought so chilling it makes me sick. And yeah, thinking about Howie just stuck here forever, especially in the winter when there's no one around, makes me so sad that it feels like something is tugging on my heart.

And then Kit and I turn to Evelyn, who I just now realize has been standing here frozen in silence, staring at our cabin.

"Uh-oh," Evelyn says in stunned horror. She points to our cabin, where Helen stands with her arms crossed and her nearly yellow eyes gleaming in the moonlight.

A low growl ripples across the grass as she marches straight toward us.

I flinch, and pull Evelyn and Kit to me, expecting Helen to devour us in a total bloodbath.

Helen practically charges toward us and then stops so abruptly and so closely that her nose is mere inches from mine. "You three are coming with me."

"What is that putrid stench?" Sylvia demands as we're herded into her Lotus tent.

Kit grimaces but doesn't fess up to her pocketful of garlic.

Sylvia sits in an egg-shaped wicker chair with her legs crossed like we've interrupted her mid-meditation. Next to her is a table with a tall metal cup and red-stained glass straw. I can't help but wonder which unsuspecting camper she's sipping on.

Behind us, Helen doesn't at all bother being gentle when

she pushes down on each of our shoulders so that we're sitting on the floor of the tent with Sylvia hovering above us.

Well, I guess one way to find out where Birdie and the missing campers went is to go missing ourselves.

Sylvia clacks her red fingernails together in a sinister rhythm. "Now, Helen tells me you all were caught outside of your cabin past curfew. Is that true?"

I swallow back my nerves. "Yes."

She takes a long sip from her drink until she drains her cup and her straw makes that scraping noise as it drags along the bottom. "You girls know I take the rules very, very—"

"We must punish them," Helen interrupts from where she lurks behind Sylvia. "Severely."

How can someone so small be so scary? Like, I'm pretty sure her feet are small enough to still wear kids' sizes.

"If you're going to make us disappear, just get it over with," Kit blurts out.

My eyes practically bulge out of my skull. "Maybe don't give them any ideas," I whisper.

"We have plenty of ideas," Helen says, her voice slithering. "Don't you worry, dearies."

Beside me Evelyn's hands are balling into fists, and I think I am well and truly scared of whatever might come next.

Sylvia says nothing as she shares a look with Helen, and then after a long moment of silence, the two of them burst into chaotic laughter that is so unsettling it makes my stomach turn.

"Don't you think the evil laughter is sort of overkill?" I ask through gritted teeth.

Sylvia looks to me with disgust for a long moment, before finally speaking. "Disappear? My darling campers, no one is going anywhere." Her words are less reassuring and more ominous.

Evelyn's body relaxes just a little, but I trust Sylvia just about as much as I like her, which is not very much at all.

"Then what are you going to do to us?" I ask, trying my best to sound more annoyed than terrified. We can't let them know that we know, because the moment they do, then we're in real danger.

She smiles, and I swear her teeth look sharper than I remember. "Punish you three, of course." Sylvia's gaze travels to Evelyn, who looks from me to Kit, her pulse jumping in her neck. "So nervous, sweet Evelyn," she tells her. "I can practically hear your beating heart."

The three of us suck in a breath.

"Tomorrow after lunch, you'll report to the camp office for your punishment."

We exhale in unison.

". . . Which you will do every day until dinner for the rest of your time here," Sylvia continues. "Now, on your feet. Helen will escort you all back to your cabin, where you will be safe and sound." Those last words come out like knives.

Helen smiles, and then licks her teeth.

As we line up to walk back outside, I turn to Sylvia. "But what about rehearsal?"

She lets out another one of those laughs that makes my skin crawl. "Oh, you won't need to worry about that. I'm removing you all from the production immediately."

My first thought is Logan, and the rest of the cast. We're only days away from Parents' Day—if it even happens at all. But my second thought is entirely selfish. I've worked so hard for the last two weeks, and a small part of me thought that this might actually be the time when I don't totally flop, but I guess I'll never know now. "But Sylvia, the show is in just a few days. What about the cast and—"

"This is what happens when you break the rules, Maggie. Not only do you let yourself down but also the people who rely on you." She shakes her head. "Your parents will be so terribly disappointed in you. But I suppose that's nothing new for any of you, is it?"

CHAPTER TWENTY-SIX

"I can't believe you're not going to be in the musical," Logan says, his voice full of agitation and a little bit of anger, as he twirls a fork through his beet salad. "What were you guys even doing out past curfew?"

I look to Kit and Evelyn for a little help, but they're both distracted by Steve, who is trying and failing to get the cafeteria staff to film a TikTok.

"I wanted to see if the ghost story about Howie was real," Evelyn says, taking the fall. "So, really, it's my fault we snuck out."

"Not completely," I add. "I'm so sorry, Logan."

"You know William and Sloane gave your role to Isabella. Do you even know how big her head is?" He stabs his fork into a beet. "I didn't think this place could get any worse, and then you had to go and—"

"Have you heard anything from Hudson yet?" Kit asks in

a failed attempt to change the subject from one bad thing to another.

I shoot her a *not helpful* glare.

"Nothing," Logan says.

Evelyn and Kit both look to me, and I know what they're thinking. *Just tell him.*

But I can't bring myself to tell Logan that his brother might be in real danger when I don't actually know for sure, and there's likely nothing he can do about it. Besides, if I just figure out a way to ruin Parents' Day, then Sylvia will have no choice but to send us all home, and if she's keeping all those kids cooped up somewhere, parents are going to start asking questions.

And then there's the possibility that we're too late. . . .

"I'll be there in the audience cheering you on," I say. "We all will be."

He nods, but doesn't look up from his plate. "Sure. Whatever. Thanks."

As we walk over to the main office, we try to brainstorm some Parents' Day solutions. "Maybe we could figure out a way to make it look like the camp is abandoned," Kit offers. "Like it's the zombie apocalypse or something."

"This would be so much easier if we just knew how it worked," Evelyn says with a frown. "If Sylvia could just control our minds at the drop of a hat, she would have already done that."

Evelyn's onto something. "That would have honestly made her job a lot easier. There's got to be some kind of thing that sets it off."

"Like an active ingredient in chemistry," Kit says as we walk into the camp office.

"Here are my three little troublemakers," Sylvia says from behind her desk, Sloane and William on either side of her. "Ready for duty?"

"Ready as we'll ever be," Kit mutters.

"Evelyn, we'll have you in the office, cleaning up and shredding years of paperwork." Sylvia motions to the two filing cabinets with ceiling-high stacks of papers on top. "And Kit, you'll be working in the Blood Bank with Nurse Belinda."

"What about me?" I dare to ask.

"And you, Maggie, will be working on a very special project. Follow me. William will supervise you." She stands and beckons for me to follow.

I wave goodbye to my roomies as Sloane plops a caddy of cleaning supplies down on the desk for Evelyn, and Kit trudges over to the Blood Bank.

William holds an umbrella out for Sylvia as he escorts her to her golf cart before getting behind the wheel himself.

I begin to sit down on the back bench when Sylvia turns around and says, "You can jog behind us. It'll be good for you. Build muscle and character all at once."

My legs are already Jell-O from sprinting this morning on almost zero sleep, but I'm not about to start arguing now.

They take off down the path and I follow behind them in a constant cloud of dust.

William checks over his shoulder for me, and is constantly slowing down with a groan.

After the third time, I yell back, "Sorry I'm not as fast as a MOVING VEHICLE!"

Eventually, we pass the computer lab, which is just as spooky as it was the last time I saw it, and I definitely pick up the pace.

They take me through a small, cleared path in the same woods we were in last night. The thirteenth cabin is nowhere in sight, and the woods aren't nearly as creepy with the sun cascading through the canopy of leaves above.

Just as I'm about to ask where I'm being taken, I'm led out the other side of the woods to a clearing where there is a huge volleyball court covered in weeds with a tattered net strung across and a ginormous diving pool that is mostly empty and completely filthy.

"Here we are," Sylvia says, motioning to the pool.

"You're telling me there's been a pool here this whole time?" I ask.

"And thanks to you it will be clean in no time," she says.

William hands me a bucket and a bottle of bleach before getting out of the golf cart.

Sylvia slides over to take his spot behind the wheel and hands me a toothbrush. "Oh, and you'll need this. You can start on the tiles today."

I peer over the torn chain-link fence into the pool. The shallow end is grimy, but dry. The deep end, though, is full of murky green water that I can smell from all the way over here. "Um, is this some sort of health hazard?" I ask.

"The exposure will be good for your immune system," Sylvia says before speeding off in another cloud of dirt.

William leads me through an opening in the fence and proceeds to spray himself with sunscreen before laying out on one of the lounge chairs under a drooping umbrella. "Did you need something?" he asks.

I hold the bucket up. "Um, water?"

He points to the pool house and the locker room before tilting his head back and closing his eyes. "I hope sneaking out with your little friends was worth jeopardizing my directorial debut."

I choose not to open my mouth, because whatever comes out might just land me another awful punishment. Tiptoeing through waist-high grass, I find a water spigot between the two buildings and walk down the narrow space to fill my bucket.

There are cobwebs and the grass tickles my ankles or maybe those are bugs crawling up my legs. I hate this. I hate everything about this, so I just squeeze my eyes shut and let the bucket fill until it feels heavy.

After pouring some bleach into my bucket, I start the long, long process of scrubbing the tiles.

"It sort of sucks that this pool wasn't up and running for us to use," I say to William.

"I can't hear you!" he calls back.

"It sort of—"

He interrupts me with a very loud and very fake snore.

"Okay, okay," I tell him. "I get the message."

I scrub and scrub for hours or maybe it's only minutes. It's hard to say. The sun beats down through my baseball cap, and I sigh every time the clouds pass overhead, giving me brief relief.

Surely, Evelyn and Kit are equally miserable . . . right? Except I can't help but think of both of them in two of the few air-conditioned places in the whole camp.

And Kit even has access to primo snacks! Evelyn gets to use a paper shredder, which is so weirdly fun and soothing. My mom stopped letting me use ours after she caught me shredding a stack of math homework that I failed. I wouldn't have gotten caught in the first place if the silly thing hadn't jammed.

Eventually, I start to use the tiles to play a game of tic-tac-toe with myself. I try to think of a plan for Parents' Day, but my brain is too full of humidity and the scent of bleach.

Later in the afternoon, William drops a bottle in front of me and it lands with a *thwack*. "Hydrate. We have an hour before you're done so I can leave for rehearsal, which is going to be even more brutal than when you were in the show . . . somehow. You children never cease to amaze me with your endless mediocrity."

I open the bottle of water and call after William. "Love you too!"

I chug the whole bottle of water at once and then get back to scrubbing.

By the time I make it halfway across the shallow end, the heat is starting to make me tired, and it looks like I'm not the only one since William appears to be dead asleep with his magazine on his chest.

Surely, he wouldn't notice if I just stood here for a minute with my arms crossed over the edge of the pool and my head buried in darkness under my hat and arms.

I let my eyes close for a moment, and I think I even fall asleep standing right there until a distant voice calls my name.

"Maggie . . . Maggie . . ."

Completely startled, I shoot upright and look around.

But William is still fast asleep.

My eyes search the wooded area surrounding the clearing closely, looking for a flash of Howie's neon swim trunks. But nothing.

William yawns with his full body and stands. He gathers his magazine and walks toward the tear in the fence before turning back to me. "Are you coming or not?"

Quickly, I run up the stairs of the pool and leave my supplies in the grass for tomorrow.

As we walk back toward the cafeteria, I swear I hear a whisper in the wind.

"Maggie," it calls.

CHAPTER TWENTY-SEVEN

The next day, Evelyn groans as we stand alongside the barn. "I can't believe I'm saying this considering our food options, but I already regret skipping lunch. There's still time for us to go back and get, I don't know, a plate of beets or something."

I push up on the warped window on the back side of the barn in the hopes that no one took the time to lock it after last night's rehearsal. Since Birdie's disappearance, the craft barn has remained locked up during the day and totally off-limits to campers.

Kit holds up her backpack. "Well, I might have brought a contraband bag of refreshments."

I push as hard as I can from the tips of my toes and finally the window slides up. "As long as it's not beet salad."

"Definitely not backpack friendly." She squats and holds her hands in a web for me and then Evelyn to step in for a boost.

I curtsy and nod. "Thank you, m'lady." I wiggle through the window and then land hard on the cement floor. "It really does pay to have tall friends."

Evelyn is next and I roll out of the way just in time.

Kit tosses her bag through the window and gracefully climbs in.

"Now, about those refreshments," Evelyn says as she stands and shakes the dust off of her white eyelet shorts.

Kit opens her bag and dumps out the contents.

I sift through our soon-to-be lunch. "You weren't kidding about contraband."

"Hey, these are my Jaffa Cakes," Evelyn says. "I was saving them for a rainy day."

Kit tears into a bag of gummy worms—my gummy worms, actually. "I'm pretty sure finding out your camp is run by vampires and that if you don't do something about it your parents are going to forget you in exactly three days counts as a rainy day."

Evelyn sighs as she sits down with her package of cakes. "I suppose you're right."

I reach into the gummy worms and come out with a fistful.

"Besides," Kit tells Evelyn, "I've been dreaming of what those orangey chocolate English delights might taste like since the first day you'd snuck them in."

"What about the rest of this stuff?" I ask with my mouth full of worms.

She shrugs. "The perks of being assigned to the Blood Bank."

We sit there and devour the pile of treats until our stomachs stop growling and we're full enough to think straight.

Last night after lights-out, we spent hours trying to hatch a plan, but the closer we got to Parents' Day, the more outlandish and impossible our schemes became.

Then this morning, it struck me. We needed to get into Birdie's office. It was our only chance at finding more answers.

So here we are. Snooping in places we shouldn't be in broad daylight, because how much more trouble could we really be in?

"Kit, you're our lookout," I tell her. "Evelyn, I'll take the desk."

She gives me the thumbs-up. "I'll do the rest."

I settle into Birdie's chair and begin to open her drawers. It's mostly office supplies, half-eaten granola bars, loose paintbrushes, and a few photos scattered throughout.

Flipping through some pictures that were bundled together by a rubber band, I stumble across a copy of the same picture my mom showed me before I left for camp. Birdie with my mom and Sylvia outside their bunk.

I'm tempted to keep the photo, but instead I slide it right back where it was, because Birdie is coming back. She has to.

In the huge drawer on the side, I find some folders full of past campers' artwork and some Birdie originals, but so far, nothing is really screaming *quick and easy vampire fix*!

"The most interesting thing I've found so far is a jar of pickles and a wooden sculpture of a bear holding a banana," Evelyn announces.

"Under normal circumstances, I would say that's pretty interesting . . ." My voice trails off as I place the artwork back in the desk and feel the bottom of the drawer wobble. "I think I . . ." Pushing at the wood, I search for a way to lift it, but there are no holes or divots for me to slide my finger in, so I rifle through another drawer for a letter opener.

Evelyn comes to stand behind me, and from her perch near the door, Kit says, "Did you find something?"

I wiggle the letter opener down the side of the drawer and maneuver it until—POP! The bottom of the drawer opens to reveal a compartment with a tablet and one single piece of paper.

I hold the lined paper in my hand and run my fingers along the ruffled edge where it was ripped from a notebook.

ORIENTATION NOTES

- don't take notes . . . too late for that one
- the older they get, the more sensitive to sunlight . . .
    maybe about ten years for S
- impossible to sleep without birthplace soil
- can't stop counting
- sunlight rule applies to reflection
- really, don't take notes :(

Beneath the very brief notes are some doodles of flowers and at the top of the page is a set of fangs like a vampire is biting into the paper. There's also a design sketched of a picket fence—just like the one Birdie had been working on for the musical, but a closer look reveals that Birdie wasn't just designing set pieces.

"Soil . . . Logan told me Hudson snuck into Sylvia's trailer last week and there was a huge bag of dirt under her bed."

"Hudson did what?" Evelyn asks. "No wonder he went missing."

"I didn't think much of it at the time. . . . I just figured maybe she planted a flower bed or something . . . or maybe it was some weird energy-cleanse thing. . . ."

"Wooden stakes," Evelyn whispers.

My eyes widen as I look at the piles and piles of fencing built up on the side of the stage. "Forget crafting. Birdie's been building a war chest."

"I really hope it doesn't come to that," Kit says in a sing-song voice.

Evelyn takes the paper to look at it more carefully. "They can't stop counting? Like once they start, they can't stop?"

"Hello over there," Kit whines. "I'm trying to be a good lookout, but I'm having some real FOMO."

"It's notes from some kind of orientation," I tell her.

She cranes her head to the side. "Like a vampire orientation?"

Evelyn reaches into the drawer and pulls out the one

remaining thing: the tablet. "Do you think this thing has Wi-Fi?"

I take the tablet and flip it open. "There's only one way to find out."

Slower than the tablets at my school, the screen finally lights up and I swipe up to find—"Dang it! It requires Face ID."

Kit and Evelyn groan in unison.

I glance back down at Birdie's open drawers and then it hits me. "Wait! I have an idea!"

Handing the tablet back to Evelyn, I dig through all the photos again, searching for one of Birdie by herself, but the closest I come is her with a huge golden retriever. She's definitely younger than she is now, but this might just do the trick. "Hold that up for me if you don't mind," I say to Evelyn.

She holds the tablet up and I hold the photo as close to the camera as it can get, hoping and praying.

By the door, Kit sits with her fingers crossed.

Suddenly, the screen flashes and rows of icons appear.

I let out a whooping shriek. "It worked! We're in!"

Kit pumps her fist in the air. "We could be freaking spies!"

Immediately, I check Birdie's emails with Evelyn peering over my shoulder.

"So many emails from Chili's about free chips and salsa," I say as I scroll through endless piles of junk email from stores and restaurants.

"Maybe you should just try typing VAMPIRE in the search box," Evelyn says.

I laugh, but type it in anyway. "If only it were that . . ." The moment I hit enter, three emails pop up from the International Society of Slayers. "Wait . . . what?"

Evelyn purses her lips. "Adults have zero respect for cyber security."

The oldest email reads:

> To: ChirpingBirdie@umail.net
>
> From: Admin@TISS.org
>
> Subject: re: Contact Form: Service Request
>
> Dear Birdie:
>
> Thank you for reaching out with your extermination request. Unfortunately, our team is currently busy with an outbreak in South America and a vampire/werewolf turf war in Australia. The earliest we could have a team to you in the Midwest would be late September.
>
> We do understand the urgent nature of your request seeing as it concerns a summer camp full of children, so we would like you to consider applying for our Slayer Ordainment Fast Track Program for the low cost of $99.99. We do offer installment payments, though your certificate of completion would not be delivered until your final payment is received.
>
> The program includes an orientation and exclusive

ebook, as well as a wooden stake pattern and instructions plus a recorded interview with former vampire familiar turned slayer Brock Salzman.

Wishing You the Best of Luck,

Miranda

Administration Specialist and Professional Slayer

The International Society of Slayers: Humanity's Last Hope

My brain snags on those last few words. "Humanity's last hope?"

Evelyn snorts. "Unless they're booked."

"What's a familiar?" Kit asks.

"I heard Birdie mention familiars when she spilled the vampire beans," I tell them. "Something about William and Sloane not quite being vampires, but familiars."

Evelyn taps at her chin with one finger. "Aren't familiars like human interns basically? Like, they do stuff for vampires that only humans can do. . . ."

"And then one day they'll be promoted and turned into vampires themselves?" I ask.

"William is always holding that umbrella for Sylvia," Kit points out. "And I've never seen him or Sloane drinking out of those metal cups."

"You're right," Evelyn tells her before turning back to the tablet. "What do the other two emails say?"

I check Birdie's inbox. One is titled ORIENTATION CONFIRMATION and the other is CONGRATULATIONS! YOU'VE BEEN ORDAINED!

Just as I go to click on one of them, Kit jumps off her stool. "Hide, hide, hide, hide!"

On the other side of the barn doors, there are voices and I can hear the lock jingling.

Evelyn and I race to shovel everything back into Birdie's desk while Kit gathers up her bag of snacks.

I look up to see the window is still open. "Y'all, go! I'll make a run for it as soon as I can."

Kit tosses her bag through the window and holds her hand out to give Evelyn a boost.

Evelyn looks to me as I'm frantically trying to clear Birdie's desk. "Are you sure? Should I take the tablet?"

"They can't know we were here," Kit tells her.

"Go," I say as I slide the tablet and notepaper back under the drawer.

She nods and practically flings herself out the window followed by Kit.

I duck under the desk and pull the chair in just as we found it. Holding my breath, I watch as Kit's arm reaches up to close the window just as the door slides open. She pulls back and leaves the window open, a soft breeze blowing in.

"The dust in this place is killing my allergies," Sloane whines as the barn door closes.

"Well, I'm pretty sure we won't have to worry about

dust or seasonal allergies once we're turned," William says. "I mean, what's the point of living forever if you have to deal with pollen for eternity?"

So we were right. They *are* waiting for Sylvia to turn them.

Sloane snaps her fingers like she's applauding him. "Amen and amen."

"What are we doing in here again?" William asks.

Their footsteps draw closer. "We need to make a list of things for the tech losers to do before Parents' Day," Sloane tells him. "Birdie's nest of trash is going to have to go, of course. And we really need to take a look at the costumes for the second act."

William laughs. "For what? There's not going to be a second act. These people won't even know where they are after intermission. I'm pretty sure we could read them the instructions to a fax machine and they wouldn't know the difference."

I can hear hangers scraping against metal as they begin to rifle through racks of costumes.

"You're right," Sloane says. "But the whole Council will be here. I want to be prepared for anything."

I can practically hear William's eyes rolling as he responds, "And I'm sure they're so looking forward to this disaster of a musical."

Sloane sighs. "It wasn't so bad before Maggie went and got herself in trouble."

"Don't even think about giving that little punk any credit," William tells her. "Who knows what she could have stumbled upon the other night?"

"None of this is even going to be a secret for much longer anyway. Soon, these kids are going to find out where all their precious blood is going."

"Finally give their hopeless lives some purpose," William says with a laugh.

Their footsteps move toward the desk, and I force my whole body to freeze, breathing as slowly as I can.

Overhead, I hear papers being shuffled around.

"I always knew Birdie was not to be trusted," Sloane says. "Sylvia herself said—"

"We get it. We get it. You have impeccable intuition," William mimics back to her. "Let's not forget that Sylvia still sometimes calls you Sally for no reason."

"Sloane *is* an unusual name," she says. "My parents knew I needed a unique but authentic name. Besides, Sylvia won't forget my name when we're serving at her side for eternity." She over-enunciates that last word.

"Let's go," William says. "I have to watch that butterball scrub the pool."

Sloane laughs. "The pool? Isn't it being filled in with cement next week?"

WHAT? The pool I spent hours scrubbing is being filled with cement next week! My nostrils flare and my hands turn into fists. Okay, now I'm fuming. Not only is my punishment miserable, but it's also a waste of time.

William giggles. "I know. Isn't that just a deliciously pointless punishment?"

"Almost as pointless as asking Helen to write the email to the parents with directions for Parents' Day. She is two steps from feral. I'm surprised she even knows how to use a keyboard."

"Sylvia's trying to bring her into the twenty-first century, but if living in a windowless computer lab that hasn't been updated in twenty years isn't the most on-brand thing for Helen, then I don't know what is."

"Anyway, now I have to proof her email before it goes out tonight. Can you believe she started it with 'Greetings, Mortals'? Though, she did sign off with 'Eternally Yours,' which I found to be a perfect pun."

The barn door slides open and shut. I wait for the jingle of the lock before I make a run for the window and slither out into the grass where Evelyn and Kit sit in total shock with their hands over their mouths.

CHAPTER TWENTY-EIGHT

The next day, I grit my teeth through scrubbing the rest of the shallow end of the pool, and when I finish that, I'm instructed to lie over the edge of the deep end on the hot concrete so I can scrub the tile there. It's been three solid days of misery, but at least we didn't get caught yesterday in the craft barn and rack up even more punishments.

And all the while I scrub, my blood boils. In fact, I'm so angry I can hardly remember to be nervous of the dark, bug-infested area between the pool house and the locker room.

When I finally finish, I'm grimy and covered in sweat.

Evelyn and Kit are waiting for me outside the cafeteria and they both look bouncy, like they have a secret they can barely contain.

Once I walk up to them, they pull me over to the side and away from the entrance.

"I have an idea," Evelyn says.

I put a hand on each of their shoulders, even though all I

want to do is give up. I want to just swim across the lake and hide out at Camp Rising Star until I can hitch a ride to the airport. But I'm here, and so are Evelyn and Kit, and if there's any shot at stopping Sylvia's big Parents' Day plan, it's on us.

"Whatever it is," I tell her, "it better be good."

After dinner, we use the cover of the crowd of campers to slip next door to the office. Sneaking out at night hasn't really worked out all that well for us, so having the distraction of campers congregating before curfew is perfect.

Evelyn slides a small key out of her pocket and unlocks the door as Kit and I guard her.

"I can't believe you stole the key," I whisper.

"*Stealing* is such a harsh word," Evelyn says. "It was just sitting there in the drawer. I guess even vampires need spare keys."

I laugh. No matter how perfect they seem or how long they live, I can't help but smile at the thought of vampires having to deal with very human things. Like keys and money and driver's licenses.

"We're in," Evelyn says victoriously.

The three of us stumble through and immediately duck down so that no one can see us through the windows. The desk is fairly tidy with a big, sleek computer and a simple but pointless vase full of red glass pebbles.

"Is the computer password-protected?" I ask as we all sit with our backs to the wall.

Just then the door swings open, and the three of us brace ourselves to be in even deeper trouble.

"What are you all doing in here?" Logan asks, his voice full of accusation and a little bit of hurt.

We've barely spoken since I was taken off the show, and he probably thinks I'm ignoring him and that my promise to help him was all hot air.

"Logan!" I whisper as I tug him down to the floor with us. "Close that door!"

"What are you doing?" he asks. "How much more trouble can you even get in?"

"We're canceling Parents' Day," I tell him.

"What? How? Just because you can't be in the musical? That's not really fair, is it, Maggie?"

I look to Kit, who shrugs, and then to Evelyn, who pauses for a moment before nodding.

It's time to tell him.

Like Sloane and William said, this secret wasn't built to last.

I take a deep breath. "Vampires."

His face freezes, and the only proof of life is when he finally blinks before bursting into hushed, hysterical laughter.

After a moment, he sees that none of us are laughing along with him, and he becomes suddenly quiet. "Come on, you're serious?"

"Maggie," Evelyn says as she crawls across the floor. "We don't really have time to explain."

"Logan, you're just going to have to trust us," I tell him. "This is life-or-death. I'm not kidding. Not even a little bit."

A look of horror passes over his face. "Does this mean . . . is Hudson . . . dead?"

Oh boy. I take his hand. "We . . . don't know. I don't think so, but we don't know."

He nods, his breathing uneven as he tries to stay calm.

I turn to Kit and tilt my head toward Logan. "I'm going to help Evelyn." What I don't say that I hope she gets is: *I need you to babysit our friend here.*

She salutes us. "Tall friend reporting for lookout duty. Logan, you can help me."

His expression is blank as he just stares at the wall for a moment before saying, "Sure."

I crawl over to Evelyn, who has pulled the keyboard down to the floor.

"Are you in?" I ask. "Was there a password?"

Evelyn doesn't look up from the screen. "Eternal900. I watched Sylvia type it in yesterday."

"She was in here with you?"

Evelyn reaches up to where the mouse is and clicks on the email icon at the bottom of the screen. "Yes. She was reading something and kept saying it needed to be rewritten. As soon as I heard Sloane in the barn, I knew exactly what she was talking about." She peers up at the screen. "Okay, it should be right here in drafts and . . . VOILÀ!"

She opens an email with a picture of the Camp Sylvania

sign and instructions on how to get to the camp with details about the day. At the bottom of the email, one thing in particular catches my eye.

We request that you turn all your phones in at the camp office upon arrival. Camp Sylvania is a tech-free zone and we hope you take this opportunity to connect with your (slimmer!) children and nature. There will be a photographer on-site to record every meaningful moment.

"Wow," I whisper. "They really are prepared for everything."

Evelyn highlights the entire email and then hits the delete button. "They weren't prepared for this." She begins to type furiously and I watch in awe.

Subject: PARENTS' DAY CANCELLATION

Parents,

We regret to inform you that due to a camp-wide plumbing issue causing a sewage incident, we must cancel Parents' Day. Rest assured, your children will be able to meet you at the airport the following day and they will be so thrilled to tell you all about their very special time at Camp Sylvania.

Please take tomorrow to explore the Lake of the Ozarks, and please DO NOT SHOW UP AT THE CAMP.

Thank you for understanding.

—Camp Staff

"Whoa. You really know how to write an email," I tell her.

She twirls her pointer finger in the air before clicking send.

Relief floods my body, and Kit cheers . . . which is why she doesn't see Helen walk right in the door.

"You three," she says with a snarl, revealing sharp incisors that have never been visible before. She looks down to see Logan, who's scrambling into the corner. "Oh, and I see you've dragged another camper down with you."

"What are you going to do?" I ask. "Punish us even more? We only have one full day left of camp."

"You never seem to learn your lesson, now, do you, Maggie?" Helen says as she steps closer.

I stand up and run my finger over the desk, searching for some kind of pen or knife or . . . gosh, where are Birdie's wooden daggers when I need them?

Helen growls, and it's the only warning we get before she lunges across the desk for me and Evelyn.

"Evelyn!" I scream. "Get back!" I slide right under Helen onto the desk and topple the vase next to the computer that is full to the brim with red glass pebbles.

I roll over onto my back and Helen is hovering above me on all fours like a wild animal.

She inhales, like she's savoring the scent of me, and then a glittering red glass pebble catches her eye. She lets out a vicious, frustrated growl like she can't control herself as she jumps to the floor and begins to count the pebbles as fast as she can. "One, two, three, four, five, six . . ."

All those times I heard her walking up and down the path outside our cabin, counting to herself. It was more than just doing the head count. It was an obligation!

"Um, what is happening?" Logan asks.

"Oh my gosh," Kit says. "I can't believe that actually worked."

"What's happening is we have to get out of here!" I tell Logan as I jump up from the desk and pull him to his feet.

The four of us burst through the door and run as fast as we can to our cabins.

"How long do you think we have?" Evelyn asks.

"I don't know. There were tons of glass pebbles in that thing. I just took a chance. I wasn't sure if the vampire counting thing was real."

"Vampire counting?" Logan asks breathlessly. "I thought that was like just a thing on *Sesame Street* with Count von Count or from those Vampire Underground books."

Kit and Evelyn glance over to me at the mention of Dad's fan-favorite series.

"Everything's real," Kit tells him. "After the week we've had, trust us when we say, *everything is real*. Ghosts, vampires, werewolves. It's all real!"

"Well, we don't know all that for sure," I clarify. "At least the werewolf part."

"Wait," he says. "You're saying you've seen a ghost too?"

I don't want to overload him, but I can't help adding, "Not only have we seen a ghost, we've communicated with him."

Logan stays silent, but I can practically see the possibilities swarming around his head as we slow down upon approaching the path near the cabins.

"And since we're dropping bombs . . ." I clear my throat. "I guess I should also mention that my dad is the author of the Vampire Underground series."

And now he looks like he might actually pass out. "Oh my god. Your dad is Doug Hagen? Like *THE DOUG HAGEN*?"

I nod slowly. "He's not that cool in real life, just FYI. He, like, brews his own beer in the garage and it smells awful and he's obsessed with his herb garden and he feeds all the neighborhood cats even though he pretends they're annoying." Oh wow. A heaviness settles in my chest. I miss my dad. And my mom.

"Um, Maggie?" Kit asks. "Your dad sounds like a cinnamon roll and all, but I think we need to get moving."

"What do we do now?" Logan asks, still trying to process everything he's just learned in the last fifteen minutes.

"Go to bed," I tell him. "And don't let anyone in your cabin. No matter what. Even if they ask nicely."

His pupils widen with realization. "Vampires have to be invited."

"Exactly," Evelyn says.

"We'll see you in the morning," I say as we begin to part ways. "We'll tell you everything tomorrow. I promise."

He looks past us, probably checking to see if we're being chased, and then turns to walk up the path.

After he goes inside, we hurry to our cabin.

"Did . . . Did we just pull that off?" Kit asks once we're close enough to almost feel safe.

"I . . . think so." I open our door and let them step inside ahead of me before shutting it tight and locking up. "Who knows what's going to happen tomorrow? But for as long as our parents can remember us, Sylvia will have a hard time just keeping us here indefinitely."

"I hope so," Evelyn says. "I'm feeling pretty homesick."

Kit and I whimper in agreement.

Homesick. It's never felt so true.

But I'm going home. No matter what. We all are.

CHAPTER TWENTY-NINE

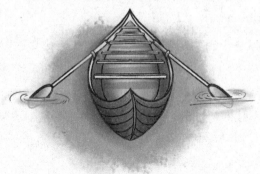

I didn't think any of us would sleep last night. I thought for sure I'd spend hours tossing and turning, trying to decide if our plan had well and truly worked. Or that I would be up all night listening for Helen to make her rounds, because she couldn't count the glass pebbles forever, could she? But the moment my head hit my pillow, I was out.

"Bryan, do you remember which cabin she was in?" a far-off voice asks.

"Tiff, if I knew, I would have said so by now."

I rub the heels of my palms into my eyes as I stretch my whole body from the tips of my toes before standing up and shuffling to the door.

Evelyn and Kit trail behind me, yawning like two very sleepy zombies.

"Did y'all hear that too?" I push the door open to find several adults wandering the paths.

"Oh!" a tall woman with long auburn curls and medium

brown skin says as she sees us standing there in front of our cabin. Behind her is a tall white guy with short black hair and a white visor.

"Do you happen to know where I can find Charlotte? She's an older camper. About this tall." She pats her shoulder. "Probably with her best friend, Tori."

My stomach sinks. Charlotte. This is Charlotte's mom and dad. Charlotte who went missing two weeks ago! Charlotte who is supposed to be *home*!

I open my mouth to say . . . something. To give her some kind of answer.

"Oh, it looks like we've got some parents on the loose!" Sylvia says as she saunters down the path with one of her umbrella handlers. "Come now! We've got a whole day of excitement planned for you all before tonight's big show, where I promise you'll be reunited with your precious children. You don't want to miss our DIY Detox for the Whole Family seminar."

Charlotte's mom frowns a little, but nods before looking back to me. "If you girls see Charlotte, could you tell her Mommy and Daddy say hi?"

I'm silent and numb. I don't even know if Charlotte is . . . alive.

Evelyn steps forward, coming to the rescue. "Of course, ma'am."

The woman smiles and takes her husband's hand as she

walks up the path and whispers, "What a darling little British girl."

Sylvia gives them a warm grin as they pass her before she continues on toward us, with Steve the cameraman a safe distance behind her, filming the Parents' Day action.

I try to push Evelyn and Kit behind me, but Kit says, "Stop. We're in this together."

"I guess this means our parents are here," Evelyn says.

My stomach twists into a knot and I can see Kit trying her best to stay calm.

After Charlotte's parents are out of earshot, Sylvia walks right up to us and she doesn't stop until she's inches away. It's uncomfortably close. She reaches out and drags a nail along my jaw. "You didn't seriously think a measly little email was going to stop me, did you?"

I swallow and step back so that all three of us are pressed up against our door. "It won't work," I tell her.

She takes a long sip from her metal cup with its glass straw. My toes curl as she dips her finger into her cup, blood dripping from her sharp, pointed nail, and then pops it in her mouth like she's just stolen some icing from the jar. "Delicious," she says, her voice practically sinful. "Stay out of my way today or I kill them all. Slowly."

Without another word, she turns and walks back up the path.

"That was disgusting," Kit says, making a face.

"Guys," Evelyn says. "If Charlotte's parents were looking for her . . . that means she didn't go home . . . and if she didn't go home . . ."

I turn to her. "She's either dead . . . or she's still here."

Slowly, Evelyn nods.

A thought begins to form as my gaze drifts across the clearing full of cabins and paths to the woods where we found the thirteenth cabin.

And where I spent the last two days. The pool. I heard my name being called through the breeze, just like that night with Howie. What if Howie was trying to show me something else at the pool? He might have more answers for us, but there's only one way to know.

"Have I made it clear how much I hate these woods?" Evelyn asks.

"You have," I tell her as I step over a fallen tree limb. "But if today goes how I hope it will, you might never have to see this place again."

"I didn't even know the camp went out this far," Logan says as he trudges behind us.

He's supposed to be rehearsing pretty soon, but as soon as Sylvia left, we went to get him. I guess rehearsals won't really matter if tonight goes as Sylvia plans.

As we step out past the other side of the woods, Kit uses her T-shirt to wipe the sweat from her brow. "What makes you think we'll find answers out by the pool?"

"Well, the first day I was out here I thought I heard someone calling my name, but I don't know. At the time, it really freaked me out, but now I'm starting to wonder if it was Howie trying to communicate with me. Maybe he has more answers for us."

"The tile does look pretty good," Kit says as I pull back the torn piece of chain-link fence for them to step through.

"It does, doesn't it? You're such a good hype girl," I tell her.

She grins. "There should be a Girl Scout badge for that."

"I still can't believe you just, like, casually communicated with the camp ghost," Logan says. "Or that he's even real . . . you're sure it wasn't just a super-windy night?"

Evelyn bats at a low-hanging spiderweb. "Unless those leaves were just really good at spelling, I think it's safe to say it was Howie."

Logan speeds up a little, so that Evelyn and Kit are a few feet behind us. "Hey, Maggie?"

"Yeah?"

He bites down on his bottom lip and shoves his fists in his pockets. "I just wanted to say I'm sorry."

"Sorry for what?" I ask. If anything, I'm the one who should be apologizing. I promised Logan we'd figure out what happened to Hudson, and here we are on the second-to-last day of camp and nothing.

He takes a deep breath before letting his words tumble out. "Sorry for being so upset with you for getting kicked out of the musical. I just didn't realize that you were only trying to help me and Hudson. And it wasn't very fair of me to be angry with you."

"It's okay," I tell him, our shoulders briefly grazing as we walk. "Honestly, I would have been upset if it was you who got kicked out of the musical. And you didn't know any of this was even happening! It's not like I could casually tell you over breakfast that our camp is overrun by vampires."

"Yeah, I probably wouldn't have taken that so well . . . ," he admits. "But I just wanted to say that you're one of the bravest people I've ever met."

I laugh, even though my insides feel warm and fluttery. "You wouldn't say that if you'd actually had to do the show with me. It's just as well that Isabella is taking my place. I crash and burn under the spotlight. It's my signature move."

"Yeah, right, Maggie. Anyone who can go toe to toe with a vampire can sing a bunch of old show tunes in a barn. Not to mention, you're good, Maggie. Even William and Sloane think so!"

My cheeks go hot with blush or maybe that's just the late-morning heat setting in. "Are you kidding me? William and Sloane would rather this musical star an old vacuum than me."

"Those two can be mean as skunks, but they made you Charlotte's understudy for a reason!"

We step out into the clearing, the sun beating down on us in full force.

"I guess so," I say, sighing. "But it doesn't really matter anymore."

Logan begins to respond, but he's immediately distracted by the decaying pool and weed-ridden volleyball court.

As we approach the pool and locker room, we find the door to the pool house is cracked open, so Kit peers inside. "No way, no how is anyone stuffing a bunch of missing people in here. This place is nothing but pool equipment, limp pool noodles, and deflated floaties."

I look to the locker room, the door of which is chained shut with a padlock. "That's what I was scared of."

"For a ghost who made such a dramatic entrance, Howie sure is awfully quiet right now," Evelyn muses.

I peer around the corner. "Maybe it's easier for him to talk to us when he's in his old cabin."

Kit walks around the side of the building and Evelyn, Logan, and I follow close behind. "There's a vent up here," she says. "Maybe we could just yell through here and see if anyone is even in there. We'll need to hoist one of us up there."

Kit and I both look to Evelyn, who's the smallest among us.

Evelyn huffs out a sigh. "Please don't drop me."

"We won't," I tell her. "It'll be like a cheerleading pyramid. Super easy. Logan can spot you."

She bites down on her lower lip. "Have any of you even done any cheerleading?"

Kit scratches her head.

Logan suddenly finds the grass very interesting.

"Not in the technical sense, but I've watched plenty of it, and I've seen acrobats do this before too," I say. "If you just step onto our thighs, it can't be that hard."

I lean against the wall for extra support and squat. Kit joins me, and after taking a few deep breaths to psych herself up, Evelyn braces herself. Logan helps her up as she uses our thighs to climb up to the vent.

"You two good?" she asks.

I swallow back a grunt as her sneaker digs into my hip. "Just peachy!"

"What do I do now?" she whispers.

"Yell!" we all tell her.

Evelyn clears her throat and politely calls, "Hello in there? Anyone home?"

"Louder," I say.

"Hello!" she screams this time. "Hello!"

"Hudson!" Logan calls. "Hudson, are you in there?"

We're all perfectly still, but the only thing we hear in return is silence.

"I don't think there's anyone in there," she says as she steps down.

Logan begins to pace frantically. "He has to be here. He didn't just *vanish*."

Disappointment weighs heavily on me. "I thought for sure we would find some kind of clue out here." Charlotte's mom flashes into my head. If she thinks her daughter is still here, so do all the other parents of the kids who have supposedly gone home.

Evelyn steps down and I sink into the grass. My eyes begin to burn with tears. This is all so hopeless. Our parents are here and they're no better than sitting ducks. We're about to disappear and become vampire vending machines.

Kit jumps as high as she can to get closer to the vent. "Did you hear that?"

"Hear what?" I ask.

Logan freezes, tilting his head to the side like it might help him hear better.

"Help!" a soft voice calls.

I know that voice.

CHAPTER THIRTY

"We're here!" I shout back as I push up to my feet.

"We're going to get you out of there!" Evelyn yells.

Kit and I turn to her, because neither of us has really considered just how we might do that.

"Hello?" another voice calls, closer now.

Logan pounds his fist on the brick. "Hudson, can you hear me?"

"We're here!" I call. "And we're not vampires!"

"Maggie?" the now familiar voice asks.

My heart sings with relief. I know that voice. I know that voice! "Birdie? There's a lock on the front door," I say. "We just need to figure out the combination."

"One, two, three," Birdie says. "Start with that."

"Is she serious?" Evelyn asks.

I shrug as the four of us race around to the front. "Am I the only one who gets weirdly stressed out when I have to open a combination lock?" I ask.

"Me too," Evelyn admits sheepishly. "We don't use them at my school."

"Don't worry," Kit says. "I've got this. I've been locking things away from my sister for years." She squats down in front of the lock and spins the dial a few times before tugging on it and then POP.

Logan rushes forward and pulls the chains off the handles, letting them fall to the floor.

"We're back here," Birdie calls from the girls' locker room.

Logan makes a run for it and I follow close behind. As I turn the corner, I find a horrifying sight.

"Whoa," Kit breathes.

On one wall is tons of equipment, much like the stuff Nurse Belinda has been using in the Blood Bank. And then lined up in a row are at least ten people strapped to hospital beds. This place is basically a much scarier version of the Blood Bank—and oof, it could really use some paint. It actually looks a lot like the orphanage set from *Annie*.

There are some familiar faces, including Hudson! And some faces I hardly remember, because they were gone from camp before I even really noticed them.

"Hudson!" Logan cries.

"Thank goodness!" Evelyn says with a sigh.

"Magpie!" someone sobs.

I scan the room. The only people who call me that name are my parents and—"Nora?" I scream in horrified shock as

227

I run to her right there in the very last bed. "What are you doing here?"

My best friend is in tears and her clothing is dirty—the same outfit I saw her in during my first week here.

"They caught me . . . that first week," she says. "And I've been here ever since. They—They made the staff at Camp Rising Star think I'd gone home because I was homesick and they've been emailing my parents pretending to be me . . . and—and I was so scared you'd never find me."

I throw my arms around her and I haven't felt so at home in weeks. Suddenly things don't feel quite as impossible with her by my side, but most of all I feel so awful that she's been here all along right under my nose. "I'm so sorry," I tell her as endless guilt boils up inside of me. "I'm so sorry you got wrapped up in this."

She sniffles. "It's okay. It's not your fault. But Maggie?"

"Yeah?"

"Do you think you and your friends could help us all with these straps?"

I smack my palm to my head and motion for Evelyn and Kit to get to work as I loosen the straps around her wrists and feet. "Have they just had you in here in these beds? All of you?"

"They let us walk around for a few hours a day," Birdie says as she rubs her wrists. "In shifts, of course. And only to keep our circulation going."

"You really didn't know about this out here?" I ask Birdie.

She shakes her head. "I only knew about Sylvia's plans to build her own little factory on this side of the camp. But yeah, I've been trying to break us all out of here."

I smirk. "I guess they didn't cover escaping a vampire's locker room lair in orientation?"

Birdie lets out a dry chuckle. "Yeah, turns out the International Society of Slayers is just as much of a pyramid scheme as my sister is."

"Your sister?" Hudson asks as he sits with Logan, their arms slung over each other's shoulders.

I help Nora to her feet, and she wobbles for a second before steadying herself. "Sylvia and Birdie aren't just sisters. They're twins."

Charlotte scoffs. "You've been locked in here with us for a week now and we're just now finding out your sister is the Whole Foods Spawn of Satan?"

"Actually," Birdie says, "Whole Foods stopped stocking her protein powder after too many health violations at her distribution plant. But yes, Sylvia is my twin."

"Charlotte," I say as I rush over to her. "Your mom and dad are here! It's Parents' Day and they're looking for you."

Her thick brows scrunch together like little caterpillars. "Wait. So does that mean they were going to release us today? They just kept us here so we didn't tell other campers?"

"Is that why you're all here?" Evelyn asks as she takes in our dingy, moldy surroundings. "Because you found out this place was run by vampires?"

Tori shrugs. "Not on purpose. Charlotte and I were just trying to sneak across the lake one night. We just wanted to see if Howie Wowie would appear, but then—"

"We saw Helen sinking her teeth into some poor fisherman whose pontoon boat had broken down," Charlotte finishes.

Hudson shakes his head. "And I saw Sylvia turn into a bat."

My jaw drops. "What did you say?"

He clears his throat. "I said I saw—"

"I think she heard you," Kit tells him. "We just need a minute to process the whole bat thing."

"Hang on." Tori holds up a hand. "All of our parents are really here?"

Birdie plops back on the edge of her hospital bed. "This isn't good news, gang."

"Captain B's right," I say. "Sylvia's big plan is to make our parents forget who we are so she can keep us here forever."

"How do you know about her plan?" asks Birdie. "Actually, never mind. That doesn't matter."

Hudson's eyes go wide with horror. "She can just do that? She can just control people's minds?"

"It's okay," Logan tells him. "We won't let that happen. I mean, we can't, right?"

We all look to Birdie. "Yes . . . and no. She *can* control people who have sipped her blood."

"Ohhhhhh." So we were right. She can't just control people's minds on command.

"So she's just going to line these people up and make them suck her blood?" Kit asks.

"The smoothies," Birdie explains.

Evelyn gasps. "We've been drinking her blood this whole time?"

Birdie stands and paces in front of the beds. "No, thank God. That would actually be disastrous. Thankfully she's only one person—or vampire, actually—so she can't just dole her blood out all willy-nilly. But she can put a drop of blood in every single one of the smoothie samples being served to your parents tonight during the intermission."

I hold my chin as a memory begins to form. "That's why William and Sloane said the second half of the show didn't matter."

"Exactly," Birdie says.

"The garlic!" Kit practically shouts.

We all turn to her with a confused look.

She moves her hands in circles, like that just might help the words in her brain come out of her mouth faster. "The wild garlic. We found a patch of wild garlic in the woods. Maybe if the whole vampires-and-garlic thing is true we can use the garlic to destroy the smoothie samples?"

I turn to Birdie. "Is it true? Are vampires allergic to garlic?"

She bites down on both of her lips so that they disappear before she finally says, "They didn't actually cover that in my orientation."

Kit's shoulders slump in defeat.

"But it couldn't hurt to try," Birdie tells her. "The one thing I've learned in the last few months since my sister turned into a vampire—okay, wow. That's very weird to say out loud. Anyway, the thing is there's all this folklore out there about vampires and I'm starting to learn that even if something isn't fully true, there's a little bit of truth in everything."

Evelyn goes into full stage-manager mode as she pulls a notebook out of her backpack and begins to write. "Okay, Kit, you're in charge of the garlic. We need some volunteers to go with her."

Kit shakes her head. "We need to pick as much as we can."

Charlotte and Tori raise their hands.

"All of us can help," Hudson says.

"We need all hands on deck," I tell him.

Logan smiles apprehensively beside Hudson.

"Sylvia's planning on giving a speech during intermission," Birdie tells us. "That's when she'll make her move."

"So someone needs to distract her while we destroy her smoothie samples," I say.

Nora grins. "I think we can handle that, right, Magpie?"

"Heck yes, we can!" I give her a high five before turning back to Birdie. "Do you think this could actually work?"

Birdie plants her fists on her hips, and for a second, she looks like she could save the world. "I don't know, but I'm going to fix this. I'm going to fix all of Sylvia's messes. I'm done letting her ruin this place."

"Now you're sounding more like a slayer," I tell her. "Oh. One last thing: How did you know the combination to the lock?" I ask.

She laughs. "I didn't, but I did know that Sloane and William—Tweedledee and Tweedledum—were in charge of changing it every few days. I figured it had to be something simple. My second guess was 911."

It takes a few minutes to make sure everyone is on their feet and ready to go, but eventually, we file out of the locker room. They all squint and shrink under the sun, like they haven't been outside in ages, and I guess they really haven't.

Evelyn, Kit, and Hudson split off with most of the group and head toward the patch of wild garlic while me, Nora, Birdie, Logan, and a few others head toward the craft barn to make a plan for tonight and hopefully scrape up a few weapons from Birdie's woodshop.

"Captain B?" I ask. "What if this doesn't work? We can't just wait for the International Society of Slayers to return from the outbreaks they're dealing with."

"So you saw that too?" she asks. "Rather than lecture you about privacy, I'll just say I'm impressed with your detective work." Her voice drops as she whispers, "And I don't know. I'm sorry. I know that's disappointing. When I was your age, I thought the adults around me had all the answers. I thought that even when things felt scary or dangerous, that the adults in my life would catch me."

I nod along, because it's true. I'll never forget the crushing disappointment I felt when Mom and Dad told me they were sending me here and it only got worse once I got to this place and at every turn, it was way more awful than I could have ever imagined. At least I got two new best friends out of the deal. . . .

"I'll always remember the moment I realized the adults in my life didn't have all the answers," she continues. "They just got better at making it up as they went along. Because that's what we're all doing, Maggie. Most of us are trying as hard as we can. For the most part, we're just winging it."

I take a deep breath, letting the lush forest fill my lungs. "Well, if I'm going to wing it with anyone, I'm glad it's with you."

She smiles. "The feeling is mutual, Maggie Bananas."

CHAPTER THIRTY-ONE

"You really think we can pull this off?" I ask Nora. "You weren't even in the Camp Rising Star acrobatics class for more than a few days. And I only did tumbling classes for half of fourth grade."

"Madame Veronica said I'm a natural aerialist," she assures me. "And I'm sure you are too. Plus, if we do our jobs right, no one will do any flying through the air."

That doesn't stop my stomach from gurgling at the thought of what we're about to do tonight. I hand her one of the old beat-up helmets I found in the trunks backstage. "Maybe we should wear these. Your parents are already going to freak out when they find out you were kidnapped by vampires."

"About that," she says. "Do you think it's the wisest decision to just spill the vampire beans to a roomful of adults?"

"Why not?" I ask as I rifle through a trunk labeled *TALENT SHOW PROPS* while we sit backstage just an hour or so before the cast will be trickling in followed by a horde of eager parents.

She wraps a red feather boa around her neck. "Will they even believe us? How many times did you tell your parents you didn't want to be here and they ignored you?"

"So many times."

"And in third grade, I had to tell my parents that my lunch was being stolen six times before they went up to the school to deal with it. I love our parents. Especially when your dad makes Dutch pancakes for breakfast, but sometimes adults only hear what they want to hear."

She's right. I know she is. And what would adults even do about vampires? Call the police on an immortal species that could probably kill us all in a flash?

I poke my head out from the side of the stage. The barn is full of rows and rows of benches. At the back is a small but ominous stand with a sign that reads CONCESSIONS. Running my fingers along the red velvet curtains, I can't help but feel a little excited. This is definitely not the show I planned to star in, but there's that fluttering feeling I get before a school play or choir concert.

Nora plucks out a pair of fairy wings and tosses them to me. "It can't hurt to look the part . . . right?"

I gasp with delight as I pull them on. "If we're going to defeat a vampire, we might as well look fabulous doing it."

The barn door slides open.

"I think that's them," I whisper.

Nora nods before flinging herself into the trunk and closing the lid. "Say 'pooping goose' if you need me."

I step out onto the stage as Sloane and William walk in with Logan just a few feet behind.

Logan gives me a soft salute before shutting the barn door behind him.

William jumps back a little at the sound of the shutting door.

We've got them right where we want them, and it honestly feels weirdly nice to finally be the one making my counselors uneasy.

"What exactly do you think you're doing on that stage, young lady?" Sloane asks.

"I'm so glad you're here," I say breathlessly. "We didn't know what to do."

Behind them, Logan flashes a quick thumbs-up. After his reunion with Hudson, I'd asked for his help in luring Sloane and William here. The rest would be up to me and my hopefully stellar acting skills.

"Drop the dramatics," William said. "You skipped your work duties today and your morning workout. Trust me, just because your parents are here doesn't mean you're not going to pay the price."

"You've seen my parents?" I ask, because I can't help myself. Everything has happened so quickly over the last few days that I'd somehow managed not to think too much about the fact that my parents would be *here*. Finally. But instead of them rescuing me, it's me who's rescuing them.

"Yes," William tells me. "And they're nearly as dull as you are."

"Ooooh, burn," I say.

He rolls his eyes. "So what's the problem?"

I begin to hyperventilate—just a little. "I was in here . . . because I was just so sad about not being in the show tonight, so I just . . . I had to come say one last goodbye to the set and to just soak it all in—"

"We get it," Sloane deadpans.

"Okay, so I went into the fitting room and I found Helen . . . except some awful person had tied her up . . . and it kind of smelled like garlic in there for some reason. But she was fast asleep! Logan came in then and we tried to wake her up, but she was basically unconscious."

William and Sloane share a panicked look with each other before racing across the barn and onto the stage.

Logan holds his hand low for a baby high five and we chase after them.

The two of them storm into the dark dressing room and through the double doors. It takes them a moment to turn on the lights and see that—

"There's no one in here . . . ," Sloane says, puzzled.

"Where'd did she go?" William asks. "Helen?"

"Now!" I yell.

Logan pulls the door shut, and I take the heavy chain from the pool locker room and loop it through the handles.

"Grab the lock," I tell him.

He runs over to where the lock sits next to the trunk that Nora is hiding in.

William and Sloane bang against the door, and if I weren't bracing myself, I probably would have toppled backward.

"I can't hold this for much longer," I say just as Logan, with trembling hands, loops the lock through the chains and clicks it shut.

We both give each other a long look before easing up and quietly stepping backward.

For a moment, everything is perfectly still.

Nora opens the trunk and tiptoes toward us, taking my outstretched hand.

"Maybe they're giving up?" Nora whispers.

"Or maybe they're plotting their escape?" Logan offers.

The doors shudder and rattle as something or someone is thrown against them.

"The costume wardrobe," I say, pointing to the tall wardrobe behind the stage manager's desk where all the costumes are stored. "Maybe we can push it in front of the doors?"

"And what are we supposed to tell the cast when they find out the dressing room is off-limits?" asks Logan.

"A termite infestation," I tell him. "That sounds thoroughly gross and believable to me. And it's half-true. We do have an infestation. Of the bat variety. Come on. Let's move this thing."

On the other side of the doors, Sloane and William continue to try their luck as the three of us grunt and groan while we slide the heavy wardrobe in front of the doors.

Once the wardrobe is finally in place, all you can hear is the occasional rattling.

"Did anyone hear that?" I ask.

"Hear what?" Nora responds with her own slightly evil laugh.

CHAPTER THIRTY-TWO

"How's it going with the garlic picking?" I ask as Birdie carries the giant wooden ladder across the barn and places it under the rafters at center stage.

"Good. Evelyn has everyone peeling and smashing up the garlic." She eyes me in my fairy wings. "I can't believe I'm letting you two climb up there. Your mom is going to kill me."

Kit cracks open the barn door and slithers in before sliding it shut. "Is it possible to lose your sense of smell from overexposure? The inside of my nose is basically numb from all that garlic."

Birdie's forehead wrinkles with worry. "This is so, so bad. I can't believe I let it get to this point where I'm sending two campers—"

"Technically I'm a Camp Rising Star camper," Nora reminds her.

"Right," Birdie says as the worry in her brow deepens. "That might make it worse."

We need Birdie and we need her in a good headspace. My brain is full of a million doubts and questions, but I can't let myself stop and pay attention to them. And neither can she. "Birdie. Look at me," I tell her. "We can't change the past. We can't change how or why you, Sylvia, and the rest of us got here. But we can do our best. And we have to, even if it's not perfect, because it's our only shot. Even if it's scary. The thought of not even trying scares me the most."

She takes a deep breath in through her nose. "You're right." She steadies the ladder. "Kit, I hope you're as good with knots as you are at spotting wild garlic."

Kit takes one of the ropes Birdie discovered this afternoon. "I've got the Girl Scout badges to prove it."

Nora and I trust Kit's process and Birdie's watchful eye as they both use rope to create a harness that wraps across our chests, under our arms, and around our waists. Hopefully these are nothing more than a safety measure, because it's not like we've had time for a dress rehearsal.

Nora takes to the ladder first, and I'm so impressed by how quickly and fearlessly she scurries up to the rafter and sits with her feet dangling.

"You got this, Maggie Bananas," Birdie whispers.

The ladder creaks beneath my weight as I pull myself up. Every bad thing that could possibly happen runs through my brain. This rickety old ladder breaks. We fall. Kit's knots don't hold. Or specifically, they don't hold me, because I'm fat and maybe fat kids aren't meant to test the boundaries of gravity.

But I step up one foot at a time, and eventually I reach Nora, and her smiling face is waiting for me as I awkwardly maneuver from standing on the ladder to perching on the beam.

I sit there and take in the view below. "This is pretty cool."

"You okay up there, kids?" Birdie calls.

We give her the thumbs-up, and Kit with her backpack on climbs the rungs of the ladder so she can tie our ropes to the beam. Her tall body stretches so far up the ladder that I feel like she only has to go halfway up before she reaches us.

Once she ties off our ropes and triple-checks her knots, she reaches into her backpack and hands us each a jar of salt with a metal lid that pops open for pouring.

After Kit heads down and Birdie puts away the ladder, they both disappear, and the cast of the show slowly starts to trickle in.

I turn to Nora, who holds her hand out for me.

"And now," I say, "we wait."

It's a long hour and a half before parents begin to make their way inside. The sun casts lengthy shadows across the floor of the barn as it begins to set.

"Maggie," Nora whispers. "There they are."

I lean over to get a better look, and Nora's right. There they are. Mom is wearing her favorite sundress, ruffly straps with thin blue and white stripes. And Dad is in his nice khaki shorts and the blue polo Mom always asks him to wear on Easter—totally not his normal jeans and band T-shirt style. Their eyes search the whole barn, looking for me. Most of the campers except for the cast and crew were allowed to reunite with their parents during dinnertime, but I've been up here.

Mom and Dad whisper to each other as they point to a section of benches near the front.

A lump catches in my throat as I lift my arm and wave even though they can't see me. I've felt so many things about my parents over the last few weeks. I've been angry. I've missed them. I've been scared for the future. But seeing them now is such a comfort and suddenly this whole nightmare being over feels more possible than ever.

Behind the rows of benches, Steve begins to set up his camera equipment, but Sylvia quickly shoos him away. Whatever's about to happen tonight, she doesn't want recorded.

Hudson sneakily trickles in with his grandmother and even Tori and Charlotte slip in with their parents, doing their best to go unnoticed.

This feels so normal that I can almost taste victory.

But it's not normal. None of this is.

"Nora, I ruined your summer," I tell her as we let our feet swing back and forth. "You've been cooped up here for two weeks when you could have been at the summer camp of our dreams."

She shakes her head. "I don't know what kind of mental

gymnastics it took for you to decide this is all your fault, but I'm pretty sure you didn't turn Sylvia into a vampire, so you're definitely not to blame." She leans her head on my shoulder. "Is it how I dreamed of spending the first weeks of summer break? No. Would I do it again if it meant we'd have the chance to take down Sylvia together? Probably."

"I'm going to make it up to you," I tell her. "When we get home, we're making every day count. We're living it up. The pool with the good waterslides, the arcade with that broken game that just spews out tickets, the place that sells those cream puffs with strawberry filling, the stationery store with those cute little highlighters you love—we're doing it all."

"Trust me, if we survive this, we're going to be celebrating nonstop. But it's not every day you get to save the world—or at least a camp—with your best friend."

And she's right. The one thing I don't like about all the horror movies Dad watches is that, in the end, it's always down to one last person to save the day. But it's not like that in real life. Heck, it can't be. If I had to do this alone, we'd all be vampire fountain drinks by now.

Just below us, behind the curtain, Sylvia storms backstage. "Where are Sloane and William?" She sounds more frantic than I've ever heard, and nothing like the eerily calm energy she normally portrays.

Logan steps forward. "They were here a little while ago, but they both started to feel sick . . . something about the beet salad."

Sylvia crosses her arms and purses her lips. "I suppose the show must go on. Are you all ready?"

Logan nods.

"Well, good luck then."

Some of the cast members gasp, and so do I. There are some things you just don't say in theater, especially on opening night!

Logan clears his throat. "Um, ma'am, Sylvia, with all due respect, you're not supposed to say the *L* word backstage. It's a pretty serious superstition. That's why we say 'Break a leg' instead."

Sylvia shrugs. "Sure. Fine. Break your legs for all I care."

She walks off, back out into the crowd, and Logan briefly glances up to us with a wink.

"Talk about a cutie," Nora whispers.

"Not you too," I tell her.

She snickers.

Somewhere backstage, a loud crash sounds, like someone ran into one of the prop drums, and then comes a howling noise that ends in a screech.

"Uh, that didn't sound good," Nora says.

I peer over my shoulder and beyond Nora to try to get a look at what happened, but it's too dark.

Then Logan rushes out onto the stage in his Mario the Librarian costume—khaki pants, a button-up shirt, and an argyle sweater vest. "Uh, Maggie?" he asks. "How do you feel about going on as your understudy's understudy? Isabella just sprained her ankle."

I gulp so loudly I'm pretty sure the whole audience can hear it.

After a second, I open my mouth to answer, but nothing comes out.

Nora takes my hand. "She feels great about it," she tells him.

"I do?" I ask.

Nora tightens her grip. "You got this, Magpie. And if you get nervous, just look up. I'll be right here."

From down below, Logan holds his hands together. "Please, Maggie. I can't go out there without you."

"Okay," I say, nodding in an attempt to psych myself up. I have to admit that, in a way, I was relieved when Sylvia kicked me out of the show. All the jittery stage nerves disappeared. But I let Logan down once and I won't do it again.

Out in the audience, the barn lights begin to dim. I guess it's showtime, baby.

CHAPTER THIRTY-THREE

After I agreed, Logan ran out in front of the curtain and explained our situation to the audience. "We should be ready to go in just a minute!" he promised the crowd.

With the help of Evelyn, Kit brings the ladder back out for me and I shimmy down as discreetly as possible, but leave my rope harness up with Nora.

"Don't worry," Kit tells me as my feet touch the floor. "Everyone is backstage either freaking out with nerves or crowding around Isabella."

"I just need to get back up there after intermission as fast as possible," I tell them both.

"We'll figure it out," Evelyn says. "I'm on the case."

As they scurry away with the ladder, I give Nora one last look.

She blows me a kiss. "Break a leg, bestie," she whispers.

Kit helps me piece together my costume. Some of

Isabella's things fit, but others—like the pants—are a no go, so we make it work with what we can find.

"Places!" someone calls after a moment.

The crew runs out to the dark stage, carrying the train they made out of foam board, and the fence is perfectly lined with Birdie's white pickets—or wooden stakes. Depending on how you look at it. The way I see it is those things are our insurance policy if everything goes upside down tonight.

I step into the wings and Logan pats my shoulder before running to the other side of the stage where he first enters. "I'll see you out there," he says.

As the curtain opens and the stage lights come up, I take a deep breath.

Adelaide, in her conductor costume, stands next to the train as *toot-toot* sounds crackle through the speakers. On benches meant to look like train car seats, kids in business suits sit reading newspapers and playing card games.

"River City Junction—River City, next stop!" Adelaide calls.

That's my cue.

My heart stammers in my chest.

My feet might as well be made of concrete.

Out in the audience, whispers begin to circulate as the silence on the stage becomes louder and louder.

"River City Junction—River City, next stop!" Adelaide calls again.

From the other side of the stage, Logan motions to me as Nicolette and the rest of the chorus wave at me to go onstage.

This is the moment when I choke. This is the moment when I realize once and for all, I'm not built for the spotlight.

But then I see Logan again and I remember what he said just earlier today. I am brave. If I can stand up to a vampire, I can handle walking out onstage and holding my head high like I was born for this.

I look up to Nora, sitting on the beam above the stage right where I left her. She's perched there like she could just swoop in and save me from this epic embarrassment. But Nora can't step in and take over my role. I'm the one who went to practice every day and memorized my lines by flashlight every night.

I glance up again and her smile is broad and full of warmth as she nods encouragingly.

"River City Junction—River City, next stop?" Adelaide calls again, but this time she says it more like someone answering a phone call from an unknown number.

I run out onto the stage, my suitcase in hand with *PROF. HARRIET HILL* on the front in bright white letters, and sit down on the empty bench.

Deep breaths. I can do this. I've rehearsed this over and over again.

All around me, kids start sounding off with their fast-paced salesman lines. They sing about business until one of them says, "Ever met a fella by the name of Hill?"

The passengers go on to talk about River City, Iowa, the train's next stop, and my character and how she's a con artist . . . and honestly, I can't help but think of Sylvia and all the lies she's sold our parents and millions of others.

My first big line is coming up. I grip the handle on my suitcase tighter. This is the easy part, I remind myself. Taking down Sylvia is the real show.

The fake train comes to a fake stop and I stand with my suitcase and tip my hat.

Just say the line!

One last deep breath.

"Folks," my voice booms, surprising even me. "You intrigue me. I think I'll give Iowa a try."

I catch the briefest glance of Sylvia, sitting in a director's chair off to the side of the audience, and she is furious. Her eyes narrow on me and her hands grip the arms of the chair so tightly the wood could snap at any moment.

One of the kids onstage responds, "Don't think I caught your name."

I bounce my eyebrows up and down and give the most devilishly charming smile of all time before flashing my briefcase with my name spelled right there across the front.

To my delight, the audience erupts in laughter, and I make a mad dash off the stage as all the passengers realize it was me they were talking about all along.

"You were great!" Kit squeals as she helps me with my props.

I let out a soft, giddy squeal. "I was, wasn't I?"

As the curtain closes on the first act, the audience breaks out into wild cheers, and the adrenaline pulsing through my veins is so thrilling that I nearly forget what I'm about to do.

Logan rushes over to me, our bodies colliding in a big, sweaty hug. "You killed it!"

My cheeks hurt from smiling and my brain feels like it's about to short-circuit until Kit pulls me off to the side.

"Do you have any experience with tightropes?" she asks.

I hold my chest as I slowly compute what she's asking me. "Other than the one in my school playground, not much. How come?"

"Okay, well, Sylvia's about to take the stage and you have about thirty seconds to get up that ladder." She points to the ladder I just used earlier, but now it's in the dark and off to the side of the stage. "And back up to Nora. We thought we might have time to get you up there right onstage before Sylvia, but as you can see . . ."

I follow her gaze to where Sylvia stands in the opposite wing with her eyes closed like she's meditating.

I don't have time for nerves. I don't have time for second-guessing. Plus, I just killed it out there on that stage, so I basically feel like I can do anything right now. Whether that's a good thing or a bad thing remains to be seen.

Before I overthink myself to death, I scurry up the ladder as quickly as I can, tossing my hat down to Kit and Logan as though they're my adoring fans.

When I get up to the beam, I use the wall to stand up straight, and I'm thankful that this hunk of wood is way thicker than it looks. Still, I can't stand with my feet together, and if I look down, I think my knees might just give out completely.

This is terrifying. Like, the kind of terrifying that lives in the sort of nightmares that feel impossible to wake up from.

But what I've learned about myself in these last few weeks is that I can do terrifying things. The thing holding me back isn't the kids who tease me or what people might think when they see a fat girl with total star quality go for what she wants. Nope. The only thing holding me back is *me*, so I do the only thing I can do, and I take one step forward.

And then I take another step.

Out in the middle of the beam, Nora stands with my harness looped around her chest and her arms spread wide for balance. She silently nods at me and takes a step.

She's meeting me halfway. For a brief moment, the memory of our after-school sidewalk tightrope practice flashes through my mind.

I take another step. And another until we're close enough to reach each other.

"She's a triple threat, folks," Nora whispers as she pulls

the harness over my head. "Or a quadruple threat. Or something!"

I can't help but grin, and hope that this courage follows me home—if I get to go home at all. "You really are a natural," I tell her as she walks backward along the beam until we're above center stage.

We carefully sit down, taking turns supporting each other.

"Are you ready for this?" I ask.

"Born ready! I've been waiting for this moment for weeks."

CHAPTER THIRTY-FOUR

Sylvia steps out onto the stage, and the audience immediately begins to quiet. "Parents, if you'll stay seated, I have a few words to share."

"Here we go," whispers Nora.

Sylvia holds her arms out, motioning to the audience. "Now, you'll notice some camper volunteers circulating through the audience with samples of my new signature smoothie. These smoothies were created right here in our camp kitchen and include a very special secret ingredient, which I think you'll find really gives it that extra kick."

Out in the audience, unsuspecting campers line the aisles as they pass out samples in tiny little mason jars that look like they're straight out of my mom's Pinterest board.

Behind those campers, the abducted campers who were locked up in that locker room for days or even weeks follow Evelyn and Kit as they file through the crowd with very legit-looking bowls of garlic and tiny spoons as they top every single parent's smoothie with Sylvia's brand-spanking-new organic garlic detox garnish. (That one was all Evelyn's idea.)

"Now, as you enjoy your smoothies, I would like to take a moment to thank you for entrusting your children to me. Neither my staff nor myself take the responsibility lightly," Sylvia says.

I can't help but snort, and Nora shoots me a look, and I try my best to apologize with my eyes.

Sylvia pauses, her head tilting to the side like a dog who's just heard something only it can hear.

I hold my breath and squeeze my eyes shut for a second.

Finally, Sylvia continues. "I'm excited to announce that my team and I are on the forefront of some cutting-edge weight-loss techniques and wellness practices, and spending time with your overweight children has truly taught us so much about what it means to dig down deep and let the thin person living inside each of us out for the whole world to see."

Or maybe the monster inside each of us, I think to myself.

Sylvia continues on as a slow commotion in the audience begins to build.

I check with Nora. "Ready?"

She nods.

We both open our jars of salt and begin to pour a circle around Sylvia.

And miraculously, she doesn't notice at first, because

she's just as distracted as her audience is by the fact that her ice-cold smoothies are beginning to bubble—no! *Boil* over!

"Are you seeing what I'm seeing?" Nora asks.

"Parents!" Sylvia yells, panic edging into her voice. "Parents! Look at me! Focus now on me as you drink your smoothies. Don't mind the bubbles you might see. It's simply the active ingredients at work. . . . Now listen to me very carefully. . . . You are happy in your life. So happy that you don't even remember the children you dropped off here at this camp. They are strangers to you. . . ."

From the corner of my eye, I notice a few parents leaning in to her every word, but then I hear another say, "What's this lady talking about? I knew this place was weird."

"Curtain!" I scream loud enough for Logan to hear the moment we close the circle of salt, and hopefully trap her where she stands. "Close the curtain!"

Sylvia whirls around, her long, narrow fingers flexing like claws. She looks up right at me and Nora as a vicious snarl rips through her chest, her incisors transforming into dangerous points right before our eyes. With determination, she attempts to take a step, but she just stumbles back, like she's walked right into a brick wall.

Nora shrieks. "It worked!"

Off to the side of the stage, Logan yanks the curtain shut with a whoosh, but the heavy velvet drags along the salt, leaving an opening in our ring.

Sylvia sees her opportunity and pushes off the floor as she levitates up to where Nora and I sit perched on our beam.

Nora freezes and I'm so shocked that I nearly tip backward. Birdie's notes didn't say anything about *flying*!

"You," Sylvia says with a growl. "I knew I should have locked you up first thing this morning."

"We have to get her back into the ring," Logan calls from below.

Sylvia laughs. "Best of luck with that," she hisses. "And I do mean just that. Good. *Luck.*"

I look to Nora, who's still frozen, and Logan, who's stumbling backward as Sylvia zones in on him.

I may not be able to levitate or fly. Or turn into a bat. Or lose weight and be the perfect daughter Mom wishes I was, but in this moment, I can take a chance and do something that scares me, because if I've learned anything from attending a camp run by vampires it's that fear will only rule you if you let it.

Sucking in a deep breath, and setting my jar of salt on the beam, I fling myself off the edge and right at Sylvia.

CHAPTER THIRTY-FIVE

Gravity does its job and the two of us topple to the stage—well, almost. My rope is just long enough to control my fall, and just as our bodies collide with the stage, I scream, "Nora! Pour the salt!"

It takes her a moment for it to click, but she quickly flings herself off the beam and comes flying down next to me. As she fumbles with her salt, Sylvia has enough time to growl, her teeth snapping at my neck before someone tugs me back just as Nora sprinkles the salt and closes the circle once again.

My toes just barely skim the floor as I glance back to see Birdie yanking me to safety.

Evelyn and Kit pull Nora back as well, their hands frantically untying her harness and then mine. My trembling fingers tangle with theirs, but I'm too anxious to be of any help.

"Are you okay?" I whisper to Nora once I'm back on my own two feet.

She puffs out a huge sigh. "I think so. Are you?"

"I'll let you know in ten minutes," I tell her, because I'm not quite ready to believe this plan might actually work.

Birdie steps forward, pushing the four of us behind her with a white picket fence board/wooden stake in her hand.

"You don't have the guts," Sylvia tells her as she props herself up on her elbows, her normally crisp linens wrinkled and dusty from the stage floor. "You never did."

"You're wrong about me," Birdie says with ferocity. "You've always been wrong about me. And you're wrong about these kids. And food and exercise and whatever the heck wellness means. You're wrong for making money off of people who are just trying not to hate their bodies. They go to you for help and you just take their money and offer them lies and diets that don't work."

"Preach," Kit whispers, and I practically cheer, because somewhere along the way, I decided that I'm okay just the way I am. We all are.

"But mostly, you're wrong for thinking you'd get away with this."

Yes! My whole body feels like there's fire pumping through my veins.

"So you're just going to kill me then?" Sylvia asks. "Right here in front of these kids and their parents?"

"Actually," Logan says, "the curtain is drawn, so just us, and I think all the adults out there are pretty busy wondering

260

why you would serve them boiling smoothies topped with garlic."

Sylvia turns and hisses at him again, and he backpedals, tripping over his feet.

I can't help but smile. He really *is* cute.

Birdie squats down, just inches from the salt ring. "You're going to make me a promise and after you do, I'm going to open this circle and let you turn into a bat and fly as far away as you can."

"Birdie, no!" I plead. "You can't just let her go."

She looks over her shoulder up at us. "Trust me," she says. "I know I haven't been perfect, but trust me this one time."

Beside me Evelyn nods, and eventually so do me and Kit, despite the pit of betrayal brewing inside of me.

Birdie turns back to Sylvia. "Now you're going to *promise* me a few things. Repeat after me. Do you understand?"

Sylvia's gaze narrows. "Sure."

"Do you understand?" Birdie repeats in the kind of voice that would even scare my principal.

"Yes," Sylvia spits.

"Good," Birdie says. "First, you have to promise to sign the camp over to me immediately."

Sylvia shakes her head.

Birdie holds up the stake. "I will use this if I have to."

Sylvia's nostrils flare. "I promise to sign the camp over to you immediately," she begrudgingly recites.

"Very good," Birdie says. "Now. You will promise to leave this place and never show your face here again. You will also promise to put a complete stop to your vampire beverage plans."

Sylvia shuts her eyes and finally lets out a grumbly sigh. "Fine. I promise to leave this place and never show my face here again and I promise to put a stop to my absolutely genius vampire beverage empire."

With that, Sylvia stands. "You'll hear from my lawyers." And, in a moment, so fast I nearly miss it, she vanishes and turns into a flapping bat, flying in tiny circles within the ring of salt.

Birdie drags a foot through the salt, leaving an opening, and just like that, Sylvia, in her bat form, shoots up into the rafters and flies directly out of the barn doors.

Helen steps out from the shadows looking even less human than she did the last time I saw her.

Birdie immediately steps forward, blocking Helen from us.

"You'll regret this," Helen warns. "You'll all regret this for as long as you shall live." She bears her teeth, which glisten under the stage lights, and hisses. "A vampire can hold on to a grudge forever. We've got nothing but time."

But this time, I don't startle. None of us do.

And Helen takes notice as she crosses her arms and lets out a heavy huff. "Have it your way, but the Council will be hearing about this, and the Council never forgets," she says, and then in a flash, she turns into a bat and follows the same path Sylvia did.

Birdie runs off the stage and out a small side door while me, Nora, Evelyn, and Kit follow her with Logan close behind.

On the dock, five shadowy figures stand under the moonlight. As Sylvia and Helen fly overhead, the figures vanish into bats and join them.

"Was that the Council?" Evelyn asks.

"That's my best guess," Birdie says. "They won't be happy with Sylvia. That's for sure."

"Why would you just let her go like that?" I don't even try to hide the anger in my voice. "We had Sylvia right *there*. She was trapped. Now she's going to hurt someone else and we could have stopped her."

"You probably think I'm weak," Birdie tells us as she stares blankly into the space where the bats have just disappeared into the velvety blue sky. "But . . . she is my sister and I have to hope there's some bit of good left in her." She turns to go back inside. "Besides, vampires can't break a promise."

Me, Nora, Evelyn, and Kit just stare at each other, our jaws slack as Birdie walks back into the barn. Talk about a mic drop.

Logan slowly nods his head. "Live, laugh, never make a promise you can't keep."

"The sign above Sylvia's bed," I say, my memory slowly coming back from when Hudson snuck into her trailer.

"I would have made her promise a whole lot more than

that," Kit says with a laugh.

"Or she could have made her promise to get on her social media accounts and tell the truth," I say bitterly.

"Or to provide us with a lifetime supply of Lucky Charms, but just the marshmallows," Nora chimes in.

"Now that's my kind of promise," I say, my anger receding just a bit. I still wish Birdie had done more and punished Sylvia like she'd done to all of us . . . but I can't imagine what it must be like for Birdie either.

Birdie steps out onto the stage, her head held high and her shoulders squared. We all sneak out to watch her from the audience.

"Good evening, folks," Birdie says into the microphone. "My sister, Sylvia . . . has had an emergency and has left me in charge for the foreseeable future. I apologize about the smoothies. Please do dispose of them immediately if you haven't already. If you happen to be feeling any adverse effects, they should wear off by the morning. Seeing as it is the last night of camp, your kids are welcome to stay here for one final campfire this evening, but I understand if, after all the commotion, you'd rather take them with you now. I'll be down by the lake starting the bonfire if anyone has any questions. Regretfully, the second act of our show has been canceled, but please take this time to explore the grounds and visit with one another." Birdie looks out into the audience, sees us standing off to the side, and gives me the kind of look that says *I'm winging it here!*

I give her two thumbs-up that I hope says, *Aren't we all?*

The lights in the barn begin to brighten as parents stand to search for their children.

Mom looks frantically for me with Dad just a few feet behind.

I step out into the throng of eager parents and begin to wave my arms. "Over here!" I call. "Mom!"

The moment she sees me, she claps a hand to her chest and pushes through the clusters of people.

"My sweet Maggie," she says as we collide and she tucks me safely into her arms. "Did I just see Nora?"

I gulp. "Um, yeah. Camper exchange program . . . She's going to just ride to the airport with us tomorrow if that's okay." I guess it worked out that Nora was always going to fly home with us since her mom was on a work trip and couldn't make it to Camp Rising Star's Parents' Day.

"Of course," Dad says as he jogs up behind her and wraps his arms around both of us, before adding with a chuckle, "Uh, you might need to give me the scoop on Sylvia. She'd be the perfect villain for that cult slasher idea I have. Is she always that chilling?"

Mom doesn't give me a minute to answer. "Oh my, I missed you so much. And you were incredible up there, Magpie! Truly in your element! We're getting you to Camp Rising Star next summer no matter what." She loops a stray piece of hair behind my ear. "I—I . . . we didn't know that communication would be so limited, and I never should have sent you here to begin with. I doubted myself the moment you got on that plane. Ask your father."

Dad nods dutifully. "It's true, Magpie. She's been pacing the house for weeks, threatening to come up here and bust you out herself."

It's on the tip of my tongue. I very nearly say it. *You sent me to a camp run by vampires. Vampires!* But instead, the words that come out next are even more difficult to express.

"You didn't listen to me when I told you I didn't want to come here. Neither of you did." I step back and out of their arms, because it's so much harder to say this when being held by them makes me feel warm from the inside out. "You sent me here because you want me to change, but I like myself and my body just the way it is. I've done some things that I can hardly imagine these last few weeks—stuff you wouldn't believe if I told you—and I did it all in this body."

"Oh, baby," Mom says, her eyes welling with tears. "You know we've always been so proud of you."

I sigh. "I always thought that . . . but then you sent me here and I wasn't so sure anymore. Mom, I don't need to slim down for Camp Rising Star or for sixth grade or . . . for you. Just because Gram-gram made you come here and made you think you had to lose weight to be happy, doesn't mean you have to do the same to me."

Dad touches Mom's arm. "She's right. You felt it in your gut too."

Mom runs a hand across her face. "I've got a lot to learn, I know. I . . . I thought I was doing what was best for you, but I was wrong, honey. We're not perfect, but that's no excuse. Sometimes parents are just winging it too."

"Someone else you might know said something pretty similar to me recently," I tell her.

She sighs. "If you can learn to be patient with me, I can learn to be a better listener."

"I think I can handle that."

She gives me a huge smile, the kind of smile that has always calmed me and made me feel safe. Mom might not be perfect, but somehow talking to her like this, even when it's hard, makes me feel closer to her than ever.

After a moment, her gaze shifts past me to someone else in the crowd, her eyes full of memories. "Birdie?" she gasps. "Is that really you?"

I step to the side and into Dad's outstretched arm for their reunion. Birdie's grin is more carefree than I've ever seen. They hug tight, like the kind of people who can go years without seeing each other and it's almost like no time passes. Like, how I felt with Nora that one summer when her family went on that two-month road trip to Yellowstone and Glacier National Park and that place where *Twilight* was filmed. (Her mom is a self-identified Twi-hard, whatever that means.)

"Sofia, it's so good to see you." Birdie looks to me with a sweet grin. "Once I realized Maggie was yours, I couldn't unsee it. I was so lucky to spend these last few weeks with

267

her. It wasn't easy, of course. Sylvia . . . is . . . was not in the right state of mind for this. But I'm taking over the camp and things are going to change around here in a big way."

"That's great to hear, Birdie. If anyone can make this place shine, it's you."

Birdie blushes. "I'll let you three get back to your reunion. Maggie Bananas, will I see you down at the bonfire?"

"I wouldn't miss it," I tell her as she begins to backpedal toward the exit.

"Maggie Bananas?" Dad asks.

"It's my camp name," I tell him.

He turns to Mom. "Did you ever have a camp name?"

She smiles deviously before turning for the exit. "Outlaw."

"Hold up," I say. "You can't just drop that kind of info and not give me more details."

She shrugs. "Someone had to smuggle and sell all the delicious snacks from home. I was a businesswoman."

"Sofia," Dad says, his voice full of awe. "I'm impressed!"

She opens her purse and hands me a Pixy Stix, my absolute favorite Halloween candy.

"Don't ever repeat this to anyone ever," I tell her, "but I think you might actually be . . . cool."

CHAPTER THIRTY-SIX

Tonight is what I imagine camp should have been all along. The campfire is full of funny stories and scary ones too. There's even s'mores, and the way the fire crackles at its very tippy-top is mesmerizing.

Mom and Dad stick around for a while, but eventually make their way back to their hotel along with the rest of the parents, so now it's just all of us campers, Birdie, and a few remaining camp staff who have worked here for years, like the cafeteria workers, who weren't vampires but were creepy, and a few grounds people.

Nora is already becoming fast friends with Kit and Evelyn, and Birdie said she has an extra sleeping bag for her if she wants to stay the night in our cabin.

We let William and Sloane out of the dressing room, and when Birdie let them know that Sylvia was gone and she's in charge now, they stole a golf cart and fled. According to Birdie, they won't get very far. I guess their dreams of becoming vampires are finito.

Nora, Evelyn, and Kit find me sitting on a log with a half-eaten s'more in my hand.

Evelyn throws her arms up. "Let me tell her this one! Maggie, Nora is full of vampire jokes."

"I'm not surprised," I tell her. "We did a standup comedy act for the talent show in fourth grade."

Evelyn clears her throat. "Why do vampires like to scare people?"

I shrug. "You got me."

"Because, they are bored. To death!" she barely says before laughing hysterically.

I give her the biggest belly laugh I can, even if I have heard Nora deliver the same joke on every Halloween since we met.

"Okay, okay, one more," Kit says. "What's a vampire's favorite fruit?"

And this time I can't help myself. "Blood orange," I say in my best Dracula accent.

Kit groans. "You knew it already!"

"Did you know the answer to mine too?" Evelyn asks. "Were you just pretending for my sake?"

"You had such a great delivery, though," I tell her encouragingly.

Nora sits down next to me and leans her head on my

shoulder. "How are we going to explain how we spent our summer on the first day of school?"

I eat the rest of my s'more in one bite. "Well, maybe if we just leave out the vampire stuff, it won't sound so bad. We did work on a musical . . . sort of. And you learned survival skills . . . kind of. I starred in half of a show. Oh! I did swim in the lake once."

She nods. "I guess we still have a whole month to get into non-life-threatening trouble."

"I heard that Tin Roof Theatre down the street from us is auditioning for *Willy Wonka Jr.* next week."

She thinks for a moment, her pointer finger tapping her pursed lips. "Now there's a thought."

"After our tightrope act just now, I was thinking we should get our parents to sign us up for aerialist classes in the fall."

"Ya know, after this summer, I think that might have more real-life uses than you'd think," I tell her. "For all we know, we might have to escape some werewolves next year."

I glance over my shoulder to the dock, where something reflects off the water for just a moment before disappearing. "Um, hey, I'll be right back."

"Sure," she says as she sits up.

"I need one of those marshmallows," Evelyn announces. "I just put it on a stick and thrust it into the fire? Is that how it's done?"

Nora stands. "Allow me and Kit to assist with this American delicacy."

I slip away from the rest of the campers and walk down to the edge of the dock. A slow mist crawls across the water. The sounds of the bonfire are so distant and far away out here.

"Howie?" I whisper.

I'm pretty sure you can't just contact ghosts on demand, but it's worth a shot.

Everything around me is perfectly still. The water is hardly even rippling.

Maybe he's not the kind of ghost who can be summoned. I don't even know if that's how ghosts work. Still, I decide to sit down, letting my feet dangle off the edge.

"Howie?" I ask again. "I don't know if you can hear me, but I just wanted to say thanks. We never would have figured out Sylvia's big plan or put all these puzzle pieces together without you. I'm sorry you're stuck here at this camp, but—"

The water shifts for a moment, and right there beside my own reflection is Howie Wowie. His features are a little blurry, but I can see his big curly hair and tie-dyed tank top.

I let out a soft gasp as he lifts his arm to wave hello, just like he did the other night at the edge of the woods.

"I hope you're happy here," I whisper. "And I want you to know that Sylvia is gone from this place . . . for good."

He smiles, and then a strong gust of wind blows across the dock, and just like that—he's gone.

Goose bumps run up my arms, and I hold myself tight, trying so hard not to be spooked, even if Howie is for sure a good ghost.

"Were you talking to someone out here?" a voice asks.

I tip my head back to see Logan and my cheeks immediately flush. "Um, that depends on how much you heard."

He sits down next to me. "Just something about how you saved the whole camp from a vampire."

"Not just one," I remind him.

"I need to thank you," he says a little more softly. "For helping me find Hudson . . . I can't imagine what they might have done to him if you hadn't found him today."

"It wasn't just me," I tell him. "Just a little bit of luck, I guess, and maybe some accidental bravery."

"I think it was a lot more than an accident."

Biting down on my bottom lip, I let the toe of my sneaker skim the surface of the water. How is it that I feel even more nervous than I did in the moment when I dove into midair and collided with Sylvia? Or when I stepped out onto that stage?

Logan looks up at the stars, like it's easier to make eye contact with them instead of me. "Um, Maggie? Would it be weird if I said you're the coolest person I've ever met?"

My hands tighten on the edge of the dock and I let out a nervous giggle. "I guess not."

His fingers inch toward mine until the edges of our pinkies touch. "Good. I'm not just saying this because of your dad, but you're basically the most interesting person I've ever met."

I turn my head away from him for a moment and let the goofiest smile of all time take over my entire face. "Cool," I finally manage to say. "I think you're pretty great too." I feel like my whole heart is beating in my pinkie finger.

"I better get back up there," he says before standing up. "Maybe next summer we can get together and get abducted by aliens."

I snort obnoxiously. "I wouldn't joke about that kind of thing."

Logan grins. "I'll see you there, right?"

"For sure. Just give me a minute."

Logan wanders back to the fire, and my cheeks are more red than Sylvia's cafeteria for the last three weeks.

Below me, color flickers across the water and Howie's reflection forms on the surface.

I lift my arm to wave, but this time Howie is laughing as he makes a kissy face.

"Oh, come on!" I say as I kick at the water. "Have you ever heard of a thing called privacy?"

His reflection sinks back, and I can't help but laugh. Someday, if I'm a ghost, I hope I still have a sense of humor.

CHAPTER THIRTY-SEVEN

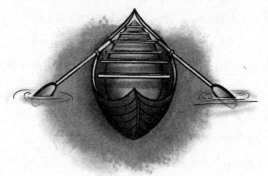

"You sure you got everything, Maggie?" Dad asks for the fifth time.

"I'm positive," I tell him. I can't find it in me to be annoyed with him after spending the last few days thinking he might just forget me forever.

Nora follows Dad out to the rental car up past the Blood Bank, which looks like it was ransacked by raccoons in the middle of the night, except it definitely was not raccoons.

I turn back to the cabin where Evelyn and Kit are still packing up. "I'll be right there," I call to Dad.

"I guess this is goodbye," Kit says.

"Not goodbye." Evelyn frowns. "Surely, this isn't good-bye-goodbye. You two both need to visit me in England. And—*and* Kit needs to take us on a real camping trip."

I groan.

"We can start with backyard camping," Kit offers. "There's still Wi-Fi. And access to indoor plumbing."

"Now you're talking," I tell her as I open my arms and the two of them come rushing in for a group hug. "Definitely not goodbye. I think after the summer we had, we're stuck together for life."

"That sounds pretty great if you ask me," Kit says.

"We can video chat," Evelyn says. "That's how me and my dad stay in touch."

"Every week," I promise.

Kit's voice is muffled with tears. "And maybe we can talk our parents into sending us all to camp together again."

"Imagine how much fun we could have at a normal camp," Evelyn muses.

"I love y'all," I whisper. And it's true. I don't think I could have survived this without them. In fact, I know I wouldn't have. Despite all that's happened, I'd do it all again if it meant counting Evelyn and Kit as forever friends.

The door lets out a long screech as it swings open and Mom sticks her head inside. "You ready, Magpie?"

"Just a minute," I call before squeezing Kit and Evelyn to me for a moment longer. "Definitely not goodbye," I tell them both before untangling myself and following Mom outside.

Birdie stands there with her clipboard. "Maggie Bananas, you are officially signed out."

I salute her. "You know, maybe you two"—I point back and forth between her and Mom—"could work on staying in better touch this time."

Mom nods with a smile as she looks to Birdie. "It's like you read my mind, Maggie."

Birdie turns to me. "You're always welcome here," she tells me. "I know this summer wasn't . . . what you expected, but I would love to have you back once I get a chance to reboot the place."

"I don't know," I tell her. "Is there any hope of the Jet Skis coming back?"

Mom laughs. "Those Jet Skis are a death wish."

My jaw drops and I clutch a hand to my chest. "You've ridden the Jet Skis?"

"Oh, my dear, the stories I could tell you," she says.

I look to Birdie. "I don't think that I could, in good faith, ever come back unless you let me take those Jet Skis for a test-drive. Right here. Right now."

Birdie stutters, "Oh—oh, I—I don't actually know the current status on the insurance with those and I do believe you have to be with someone at least fourteen years of—"

"I'll take her out on one," Mom says. She holds a pinkie out for a promise. "Any injury, damage, and yada-yada is my own fault."

Birdie looks to the docks, then to Mom, then to the docks again, and then to me before unclipping the giant key ring hanging from her belt loop. "Just one quick circle. No stunts." She holds the keys and Mom reaches for them just as she pulls them back. *No stunts.*

Mom sighs with a *humph* and finally nods. "No stunts."

Is this woman actually my mom?

"Mom," I whisper as we walk down to the dock. "Are you saying you know how to do stunts on a Jet Ski?"

She smiles. "I'm not saying I know how, but I am saying I was once foolish enough to try. Or should I say Outlaw was."

I shake my head in disbelief as I realize that my mom is full of surprises.

It takes Birdie a few minutes to unlock one of the Jet Skis and get it set up for us. She excuses herself when she notices Steve the cameraman poking around the front office. I'm sure he has lots of questions, plenty of which Birdie can't answer.

With life jackets secure, Mom gets on the Jet Ski and I saddle up behind her before wrapping my arms tightly around her waist.

"Are you ready, Maggie Bananas?" Mom asks.

"Do it to it, Outlaw."

She grips the handles and we're off, skidding across the water. Mom lets out a howling *"Woohoo!"*

Somewhere, along the shore, something howls back at her, and I can't help but laugh.

My hair ripples through the wind as we turn to head back. "Mom, how'd you learn how to do this?" I yell as we skip over a wave.

She tosses her head back with a laugh. "Maggie, what happens at summer camp, stays at summer camp!"

ACKNOWLEDGMENTS

Maggie couldn't save the day alone, and I couldn't have written her story on my own either. This book lived in my brain for a very long time, and so many wonderful people helped me dream these pages into existence.

Before I go any further, though, I would like to say that part of the creation of this book took place during the HarperCollins strike. I owe a great deal of gratitude to so many members of the HarperCollins Union for the work they've done on my books, but also for their bravery, determination, and willingness to stand up for what is right. You can learn more about the union at instagram.com/hcpunion.

Thank you so much to my friend and editor, Alessandra Balzer. Long live Birdie! (Johnny and Joey too!)

To my agent and co-conspirator, John Cusick, thank you for always being the first to say, "Heck yes."

HarperCollins has very much become my publishing home, but it's the people who really make it what it is. Thank you to Emily Mannon, Robby Imfeld, Taylan Salvati, Caitlin Johnson, Donna Bray, Suzanne Murphy, Nellie Kurtzman, Ann Dye, Andrea Pappenheimer, Kerry Moynagh, Kathy Faber, Almeda Beynon, Mark Rifkin, Stephanie Evans, Kathryn Silsand, and Veronica Ambrose.

This stunning cover was created by Jenna Stempel-Lobell, whose taste is exquisite, and I am deeply thankful to be the beneficiary of her keen eye. Thank you also to Steph Waldo for the wonderful cover illustrations and the interior map of my dreams. Many thanks to Alix Northrup for the custom letter work.

Thank you to Dani Moran, Lilian Garcia, and Jada Johnson for their valuable input.

I am so grateful to several friends who brainstormed with me and offered their support during this process. Thank you to: Mary Kole, Kristin Treviño, Molly Cusick, Holly Black, Cassie Clare, Kelly Link, Sierra Simone, Natalie C. Parker, Tessa Gratton, Ashley Lindemann, Ashley Pierce, Paul Samples, Luke and Lauren Brewer, Cathy and Valerie at Blue Willow Bookshop, and Morgan and Lee at Pantego Books.

Pamela and Frank Warrington, thank you for the bimonthly pick-me-ups via Zoom.

Thank you to Bob and Liz Pearce and Roger, Emma, Vivienne, and Aurelia Trevino.

Thank you to the Josh, Bethany, Noah, and Teagan Taylor, my Lake of the Ozarks family.

Mom and Dad, thank you for your endless love and support and for always making laughter a priority.

To my cats, Opie, Rufus, and Margo, who offer their cuddles at the most inopportune times. And to my sweet Dexter, you are forever missed.

Ian, you light me up. Thank you for always cheering me on. Let's buy a Jet Ski and fight some vampires.